My Bad Boy Billionaire Bodyguard

NOELLE STONE

Chapter One

TONIGHT'S CROWD is exceptionally energized, as if they're feeding off my own excitement. Even though this is a dive bar on the outskirts of Paris, Texas, the dangerous kind where it wouldn't be a stretch if the Hell's Angels rolled up to, I'm not nervous. Not when I'm playing my music, and even though electric violin likely isn't something this crowd listens to all that often, they're digging it. This is my final performance before hitting the road and heading to New York, where I have a chance to achieve my biggest dream…joining the orchestra at Carnegie Hall.

The bar is pulsing with life. The smooth, electric sound of my violin pumps through the speakers above and to the sides of the stage, mixing with the pop music I use to accompany my playing. The crowd cheers and moves along with me as I dance. Sweat drips down my forehead and my heart races. I'm exhausted, but the adrenaline pumping through my veins and the sheer thrill of performing are going to push me through this last song. I'll collapse after the show and sleep well into tomorrow, but for right now, I'm focused as I own the stage and entrance the crowd in front of me.

This is what I love. This is what I've always been meant to do. The rush of putting on a show and sharing my art is addicting and I don't think I'll ever get tired of it.

I drag my bow across my violin's strings with a precision born of years of practice. My instrument is like an extension of my body and I'm able to play it without having to think. Instinct and muscle memory take over as I lose myself in my music. I dance and twirl across the stage, oblivious to just about anything but my violin...

A loud crash cuts through the music. My body jerks, and my fingers falter, missing a note. My eyes snap to the bar. The room feels like it tilts as the sight of the fight slams into my awareness. Beer bottles shatter. Fists fly. The crowd near the bar is turning into a writhing mass of chaos.

"Shit." The word slips out before I can stop it. "Security!" I shout into the mic, but my voice drowns under the roars of both music and fight. The bouncers are already pushing through the crowd, but it's spreading too fast. One guy throws a punch, another grabs a chair. I see a bottle arc through the air and slam into someone's head.

Shit, shit, shit! The brawl is escalating. I don't have time to think. I need to get out. Now.

I rush toward the edge of the stage, but hesitate. Jumping down would put me right in the middle of the chaos, and I'm not ready to be someone's punching bag tonight. I scan the room, desperate for an opening, but it's all moving too fast—bodies slamming into each other, fists flying, drinks spilling.

A bottle hurtles through the air and slams into my head. Beer drenches me, the sour smell filling my nostrils as I stagger backward, wiping the sticky liquid off my face. My costume—my gorgeous, sparkly costume—is ruined, soaked in cheap booze. Fury flares hot, mixing with the panic already clawing at my chest. My bow—where's my bow? My violin is safe in my grip, but my bow...

Goddamn it, I dropped it.

More bottles are thrown onto the stage, and a few cups made of glass. Jumping around, I dodge the scattering shards, but I can't stay up here. A chair is knocked up against the stage. Maybe I can use it as some sort of shield to plow my way through the crowd to get to the door.

Before I can make a move, a blood-curdling scream pierces the air. My heart leaps into my throat as I lose my balance, slipping off the edge of the stage. I hit the floor hard, my back slamming against the stage's wooden edge. Pain explodes up my spine, but I clutch my violin close to my chest, keeping it safe. *Get up! Get up, get up, get up!* The crowd will crush me if I can't get up.

I scramble, fingers clawing at the stage's edge. My vision tunnels. The crowd presses in from all sides, bodies crashing together like a tidal wave. Just as I manage to get a grip and start pulling myself up, a shadow looms over me. My blood turns cold. I look up, heart pounding in my ears. A massive man is falling toward me, his protruding beer belly moments from crushing me.

I squeeze my eyes shut in anticipation of the impact.

Several moments pass, and it doesn't come. Am I safe? Why isn't big boy on top of me right now, slowly smothering me to death?

Finally cracking my eyes open, my heart flips in my chest. There's a tall figure above me, holding the massive man up with his back, keeping him from flattening me. My heart stutters. Who—? The man saving me—he's gorgeous. Broad shoulders, black hair, and piercing blue eyes that lock onto mine with an intensity that steals my breath. His leather jacket strains as he pushes the larger man away, growling under the weight before tossing him aside like he's nothing. He reaches down, grabs my hand, and yanks me to my feet.

Mmmm…he smells good.

Spicy cologne and what I assume is his natural musk. It's making my head a little foggy. Or is that the fear?

Wrapping his arm around me, he holds me against his firm, muscular body and his heat engulfs me, making me shiver.

"Come on," he says, his voice low and gruff.

With his hand firmly around my waist, he guides me away from the stage and toward the bar's wall, shielding me from the chaos of the fight with his body. I don't know who he is or why he's doing this, but I'm not going to question the help. As we move, he jostles against me. He's getting hit from behind again and again as he guides me toward the door, using himself as a human shield.

Glass shatters above us as someone throws a mug against the wall. My guardian angel covers my head with his arms and torso to protect me from the raining glass and beer.

"Oh, my God!" I shriek, gazing up at him with wide eyes. "Are you okay?"

He doesn't say a word and just keeps ushering me closer and closer to the door. Someone slams into him, but he braces his elbows against the wall to keep from squashing me. He grits his teeth and lets out a grunt.

Once he gathers his bearings again, he continues pushing us forward. At long last, we reach the bar's entrance. He shoves the door open and we stumble out into the cool night air. I gasp, feeling as though I've been suffocating for the last few minutes.

Holy shit…we made it! We're out! And I still have my violin in one piece.

Panting, I whirl around and meet my rescuer's gaze. His chest heaves as he catches his breath, causing his pecs to strain against his t-shirt. Now that I can get a full look at him…fuck, he's so beautiful. Why did he save me, though? Who is he?

I part my lips to express my gratitude, but before I can get a word out, he suddenly drops to his knees.

"Oh, my God!" Rushing to him, I reach him just as he starts to tip over and I'm able to catch his head before it slams into the concrete. I kneel next to him, fear stealing my breath again as his eyes close and his breathing grows more ragged.

"Hey, are you okay? Can you hear me? Hello?"

He doesn't respond or open his eyes. I run my fingers through his hair, and when I pull them away, they're coated in blood.

I cry out in alarm. When did he get so hurt? Was it the glass from the mug that shattered above us? Or was it when he was slammed into from behind?

Whoever this guy is, I owe him, big time. I can't just let him bleed out on the sidewalk. His hair is soaked and sticking to his scalp now. It's too much blood.

"Help!" My eyes dart around in desperation. Quite a few people are outside with us, but everyone just watches us with varying degrees of shock and horror on their faces. "Please! Someone help!"

Everyone continues to keep their distance, but thankfully, police sirens blare in the distance, coming closer and closer. My breath rushes out in shuddering relief.

"Hey," I say in a strangled tone as I gaze down at this beautiful man. He's really pale, like all the blood has been drained from him already. I snatch up his hand and squeeze it, relieved that it's still warm. "Hold on, okay? The police are coming. We're going to get you help. I promise, I'm not going to leave you like this. Just stay with me. It's all going to be okay."

Maybe. God, I don't know. He's bleeding so much…it's pooling on the sidewalk beneath his head. Head wounds bleed a lot though, right? Even if they aren't that bad? Shit, I don't know!

Sucking in a deep breath, I force myself to calm down. I'm panicking and not thinking straight. Reaching down, I rip off a piece of my skirt, ball it up, and press it against his head to try and staunch the bleeding.

Please be okay…please be okay.

As the police arrive to bring the chaos in the bar under

control and the paramedics follow after to help clean up the mess, I stay by my rescuer's side, holding his hand tightly in both of mine. Whoever he is, I'm keeping my promise. I'm not leaving him until I know he'll be all right. It's the least I can do for him.

He saved my life, and now I'm going to make sure someone saves his.

"IT ALL JUST HAPPENED SO FAST. ONE second, the show was going really well and I was just about to wrap up, and the next…total chaos."

The police officer taking my statement nods as he scribbles notes onto a small notepad.

"Did you see who initially started the fight?" he asks.

I hug myself tighter. "No, I didn't. Once it started I just wanted to get out of there as fast as possible."

"Understandable. And your companion? Do you know what caused his injury?"

I glance down the sidewalk where the paramedics are working on my rescuer. I give myself another squeeze as I fight against the panic still threatening to rise up inside me. I need to hold myself together, and I do by the tips of my fingers.

"I'm not sure," I say. "He got hit by a few different things. There was a glass mug that broke over us at one point, and I'm not sure how many people slammed into him from behind as we made our way out."

"What's his name?"

I blink and then shake my head. "I don't actually know. We've never met before."

"Yet he risked himself to save you?" The officer releases a long whistle. "That's pretty impressive."

Yeah, it is. It's wild that a total stranger would do something like that for me.

"All right, well, that should do it for now," the officer says, flipping his notebook shut. "If we need anything else, we'll reach out."

"Okay," I murmur. Once the officer walks away, I turn and rush over to my rescuer. The paramedics are loading him into the ambulance. Before I reach them, I spot something on the ground where he was lying. It's a wallet. His wallet!

I pick it up and flip it open to see if I can figure out his name. His driver's license is front and center, and when my eyes take in his name, I freeze.

Ethan Cavenwell.

The name Cavenwell is all too familiar to me, and not in a good way. The Cavenwell family is responsible for tearing me and my brother apart. They blamed my brother for a robbery he never committed, and because of them, I grew up in group homes and foster homes instead of with what little family I have left.

This has to be a coincidence. We're ninety miles from Dallas, where the Cavenwells live, and no son of a billionaire would be caught dead in a dive bar. I doubt any of them would risk their neck to save a nobody like me.

Yeah, it's just a coincidence. That's all. A crazy one, but those Cavenwells aren't the only family in Texas with that last name.

I look up and the paramedics have my rescuer—Ethan— completely loaded in the ambulance. One of the EMTs is about to close the ambulance doors and I rush over before he can.

"Wait!" I shout, coming to a stop next to him. "Can I go along?"

The words are out of my mouth before I fully realize what I'm saying, but I want to thank Ethan properly for saving me, and give him his wallet. More than that, I want to make sure he's okay. He risked his safety to protect me.

"Who are you to him?" the paramedic asks me.

Shit…he probably isn't going to let me go with if I tell him I'm just some random stranger who's never even met his patient before.

"I'm his girlfriend."

The paramedic arches a brow at me and looks annoyed. Damn it, I should have said I was his wife or something. He opens his mouth, and I'm sure he's going to tell me to get lost, but another EMT suddenly comes around the side of the ambulance and slaps the side of the vehicle.

"We're ready to go," he declares.

The paramedic I've been speaking to narrows his eyes at me and then shakes his head as he says, "all right, get in, but stay out of the way, got it?"

Grateful, I scramble into the back of the ambulance before he changes his mind. I slip past Ethan's gurney and tuck myself into the far corner so I don't get in the way. The paramedic climbs in after me and shuts the doors. The next moment, we're off, driving down the road toward the hospital, and I have no idea what the hell I'm going to do when we get there.

Gazing down at my rescuer, the events of the evening finally start to fully settle over me. Holy shit…how did everything go so wrong so fast? Tonight was supposed to be my last hurrah before taking off to make my dreams come true. After years of hustling and saving and growing my name, I'm finally getting out of here and going on my first tour as I make my way up north to my ultimate destination, New York. Tonight is the beginning of the rest of my life, in which all my dreams come true and I become the full-time performer I was always meant to be.

No more scrounging for tips or begging for stage time. I'm finally becoming someone people want to see and hear.

People finally know my name!

I wanted to go out on a high note in my hometown, but in an instant, the night was ruined by some drunken idiots. Sucking in a deep breath, I push down the surge of anger and frustration bubbling up inside me. This doesn't change my plans. I'm still going on tour. I'm still going to New York.

I just need to hold it together. I start compartmentalizing my panic as I remind myself of all the things I can control right now.

It's a technique I've developed over the years called, *if I can change my attitude, I can change this situation!* (patent pending).

Even if I can't control the situation around me or other people's reactions, I can control my own attitude and response.

It helps to calm me down and I'm able to look back down at my rescuer with a clearer head and more focus. One thing at a time. First, I need to make sure he's going to be okay, and then I can figure out what my next move will be.

I drum my fingers against the arm of the chair I'm sitting in and I gaze at Ethan, lying unconscious in the hospital bed across from me. It's been over an hour since we got here and he hasn't come yet. His doctor has assured me that's not unusual. He has a concussion, but at least the cut to his head really isn't as bad as it looked, and other than a few bruised ribs, he should be totally fine and will wake up on his own.

My violin rests against the wall next to me, and I feel more at ease. At least, throughout this whole disaster of a night, I was able to hold onto it. It's a small relief within a wild clusterfuck.

Sighing, I look at the beautiful man lying in the hospital bed. A part of me wonders if I should go. Even though I'm a total stranger with no connection to this man other than our encounter at the bar, I can't bring myself to get out of my chair. I haven't left his side since the ambulance; I'm even still wearing my alcohol soaked costume and platform boots. My clothes are dry now, but the beer smell has started to sour. Still, I can't just leave him like this.

As I'm staring at him, his eyelids start to flutter open. Shit! Is he waking up?

I jump to my feet and hurry to stand next to his bed, gazing down into those stunning blue eyes. He stares up at me, his brow furrowed in confusion.

"Where…where am I?"

"You're in the hospital," I explain. "Do you remember the bar fight? You got hurt trying to get me to safety."

He appears thoughtful. There's a glassiness to his gaze, and I wonder how strong the pain meds he's on are.

"Right…" he murmurs at length, rubbing his hand down his face, his eyes hooded and glassy. "Bar fight. You…you were the girl on stage."

"That's right, I was. My name is Arya."

"Ethan," he responds. "Ethan Cavenwell."

"Nice to meet you," I say, ignoring the weird feeling in my stomach at his name. It's such a strange coincidence… "How are you feeling?"

Before he can answer, the door to his room flies open and two figures hurry inside.

"Ethan!" The first of the two, an older, elegantly dressed woman with silver blonde hair, bright green eyes, and a single strand of pearls around her neck. "Oh, my God! Are you okay?"

She rushes to Ethan's beside, her hands fluttering in front of her like agitated birds.

"I'm all right, Mom," Ethan assures the woman.

I freeze. Mom? This is his mother? I frown. She seems oddly familiar.

My gaze shifts to the sour-faced older man with the same dark hair and blue eyes as Ethan who comes in behind Mrs. Cavenwell. Even if he wasn't a U.S. Senator, I would know this man anywhere.

Jared Cavenwell. The man who accused my brother of the

supposed robbery that sent him to prison and left me totally alone. Just the sight of him spikes my temper.

Ethan, my rescuer, is, clearly, one of *those* Cavenwells? An irrational sense of betrayal hit me. What the hell was he doing at a dive bar, seeing how the other ninety-nine percent live?

"What happened?" Mr. Cavenwell demands to know, his eyes flashing with anger. "How the hell did you end up in this state, Ethan? The nitwits on staff here can't seem to give us a straight answer."

I wince at his harsh tone. His son's in the hospital and he's yelling at him instead of asking how he's feeling. I'm not sure if it's the miniscule movement I make or what, but Mr. Cavenwell's eyes snap to me and narrow.

"Who are you?" he barks. "What are you doing in my son's room? What the hell are you wearing?"

It takes me a second to realize he doesn't recognize me. Blinking, I stammer, "um…I'm Arya, and…"

"Are you the reason my son is here?" Mr. Cavenwell growls.

"If you'll just let me explain…"

He advances on me, walking around the foot of the bed, and I take a few steps back, startled. He gets within inches of my face and points a finger at me.

"You're going to pay for this," he hisses. "I'm going to sue you for every penny you have, though by the looks of you, it's not much."

"Jared, the tramp isn't worth it," his wife declares, glaring at me from the other side of the bed. She's hovering over Ethan, as if protecting him from me.

What the hell is with these people? They don't even know me, and yet they're throwing accusations and threats at me. Is this what they did to Lou?

Fury bubbles up and my gaze bounces between these two assholes.

Ethan pushes himself up against his pillows, wincing as the move jostles his injured head, but locking his eyes on his dad.

"Dad, hold on…" he begins, but his mother puts a hand on his shoulder and he cuts off, sucking in a sharp inhale—she must have touched the shoulder he hit the pavement with. His father just steamrolls over him.

"What do you have to say for yourself?" Mr. Cavenwell spits at me.

My teeth clench and glare at him. I'm not going to just stand here and let these two assholes talk to me like this. That need for revenge I was feeling earlier comes roaring to the forefront of my mind. I want to make these people pay for what they've done to me and my brother and wipe those haughty expressions off their faces.

When I glance down at Ethan, a plan begins to form in my head. A way to get some payback and perhaps a payday that I could use to hunt down my brother. Making up my mind, I turn to Mr. Cavenwell and lift my chin defiantly.

"Do you really think it'll look good for you to sue your son's fiance?" I snarl.

Mr. Cavenwell's eyes go wide with shock and his mouth drops open. His wife has a similar reaction, though she lets out a startled cry.

"Fiance?" Mr. Cavenwell sputters. "What nonsense are you spouting? My son doesn't have a fiance. Ethan? Ethan, what's going on here? Is this woman telling the truth?"

We all turn to look down at Ethan, He slowly blinks and parts his lips, but doesn't say anything.

"Ethan?" his mother exclaims. "Explain yourself, right this second! Are you actually planning on marrying this…this hussy?"

I snort. Their attempts at insulting me are kind of funny. I'm in show business. I've been called a lot worse than a hussy.

However, we all continue to watch Ethan, waiting for him to say something, and I have no idea how I'm going to explain away this colossal lie when he inevitably denies it.

Chapter Three

ETHAN

WHATEVER THE DOCTOR'S have me on can't be as good at whatever this girl in the sequined leotard is smoking. I suppose this is what I get for sticking my neck out and being a Good Samaritan. All I wanted was to enjoy my last night away from my family. Have a few beers and relax. I hadn't gone to that bar for the show, but once the girl had started playing her violin and dancing around in that skimpy, flashy outfit, I'd been more than intrigued.

She might be crazy, but at least she's hot. Her long brown hair has fallen out of the bun she'd been wearing on stage and is a wild mess around her face and shoulders, and her blue eyes are wide and bright as she gazes between me and my parents. She's shorter than I initially thought, thanks to those platform boots she's wearing, and that body…she's curvy in all the right places and that leotard leaves little to the imagination.

My parents' reaction to her is also pretty satisfying.

Watching this girl stand up to my parents, no matter how crazy she is, is kind of entertaining. She's brave and bold, and I'm curious to see where she's going with this ridiculous lie.

"Son?" my father barks. "Do you hear me? Who is this girl and why is she claiming to be your fiance?"

I look between Dad and the girl and then shrug. "Because she is my fiance."

I don't know who looks more shocked; my dad, or the girl. She's staring at me with wide, stunned eyes and I have to fight not to grin. On the other hand, my father appears furious as he glares down at me, his face turning a dark shade of red.

"Are you out of your mind?" my father demands to know. "You're engaged? This is absolutely ridiculous and I'm not going to stand for it…"

"Jared, darling," my mother says in a low, firm voice. She grabs his arm like she's holding him back from me. "Now is not the time for this. Ethan is still recovering. The doctor said he has a concussion and we shouldn't overstress him, especially so soon after his…accident. We can discuss this later."

My focus is on my father. I can practically see the internal battle taking place in his mind. To ignore Mom and berate me for seemingly stepping outside of his carefully constructed plans for me, or be reasonable for once and let his injured son heal in peace.

It takes longer than it should, but he finally snaps, "fine! But this isn't over."

With that, he yanks his arm from Mom's grasp, turns, and storms out of the room. Mom releases a long sigh, shoots a glare at the girl, and turns to follow Dad.

And just like that, I'm alone with the crazy woman I saved in the bar.

"So," I begin. "You're my fiance, huh?"

She flinches and glances away from me, her cheeks turning bright pink.

"Um," she begins softly and then sighs. "I didn't like how your father came storming in here and started yelling at me and threatening to sue me. I said the first thing that came to mind to get him to back off. I'm…I'm sorry. It was a shitty thing to do."

I grin at her. "I actually really admire how you stood up to him. Most people don't. As I'm sure you realized, he's not always the warmest man to interact with."

She snorts and nods. "Yeah…he's about as warm and cuddly as a starving polar bear."

Chuckling, I say, "Tell me about yourself…Arya, was it?"

"Yeah," she murmurs. "Arya."

"What do you like to do? What are your plans for the future? These are things I should know about my fiance."

She winces again and I grin. Teasing her is kind of fun.

"Uh, I'm about to go on tour," she says. "Last night was my final performance in Paris before I'm supposed to leave. I really wasn't thinking when I told your parents that we're engaged because I'm taking off to make my way north and don't know if or when I'll be back."

That is pretty shortsighted of her, I have to agree to that. Still, I'm even more intrigued by her. I ended up in that bar because I needed an escape, and I had to go about an hour outside of Dallas to escape my father's influence. The fact that this girl is taking charge of her own life and pursuing her dreams is admirable, and I feel a small stab of envy. I wish I could do the same. I wish I could break away from the web my family keeps trying to create around me to keep me contained, but they always manage to pull me back in when I think I'm on the verge of getting free.

"Look, I'm really sorry," she says again. "Things just got out of hand. I just wanted to make sure you were okay and to thank you for helping me. I feel really bad that you got hurt as a result."

The genuine emotion in her words surprises me. When I don't say anything in response, she keeps speaking, as though she has to fill the silence.

"I, uh, I'll clear things up with your parents if you want me to," she says. "I don't want to cause any problems for you…"

"Hold on," I interrupt, an idea forming at the edge of my mind. "You don't have to do that."

She looks relieved, but she tries to insist, "no, really. It's my mess to clean up…"

"What if we didn't say anything?"

Her brows furrow in obvious confusion. "Um…what? I don't understand."

I'm warming up to the idea in my mind, even though I know it's crazy. Maybe this girl is my ticket to freedom.

"What if we pretend we're engaged for a while," I explain, choosing my words carefully.

Arya looks around, as if trying to find the person I'm really talking to.

"You want to pretend to be engaged?" She shakes her head, baffled. "Why would you want to do that? You don't even know me, and I'm going on tour anyway…"

"I'll go with you." Yeah, this is perfect. This is just the excuse I need to get away. My family won't try to pull me back if I'm out playing the supportive, protective fiance.

Dad has been on my ass for years to join him and my siblings in the family business…something I have no interest in doing. Besides being a Texas State Senator, Dad owns a logistics company based in New York that my third oldest brother Andrew oversees, and a law firm in Dallas my oldest brother Thomas runs. My brother Jesse, who is fifth in line to my family's empire, is in IT, which my father has permitted because it gives him a stake in the tech world. Finally, Victoria, the only girl, managed to snag herself an English aristocrat for a husband, so she's also contributing to the family legacy by bringing literal nobility into the bloodline.

I'm the black sheep of the family. I have no interest in serving my dad's professional, political, or personal interests and that's a foreign concept to him. We're all expected to fall in line without question and my siblings have done just that. I'm supposed to marry a girl from a wealthy family and pop out heirs to the Cavenwell name like we're some noble family from the 1700s. The only thing keeping me from shutting my dad's ambitions down for good is the fact that he's holding my trust fund hostage. No access until I meet his expectations.

Fuck Dad if he thinks I'm going to comply with his demands.

If I get married I get my money, but the choice of wife is up to me. That's the deal he made with me. We even put it in a legally binding document so he can't wiggle out of it and go back on his word. I want nothing to do with my dad and his vision for my life, and that money is going to help me gain my freedom and build the life *I* want.

Maybe this crazy girl in green sequins is offering the perfect solution. "I'll go with you on your tour."

She stares at me for several moments before releasing a bark of laughter.

"Oh, shit," she gasps. "You almost got me. God, I'm so dumb. I was falling for it…"

"I'll pay you one hundred thousand dollars at the end of the tour if you let me go with you and pretend to be engaged."

She freezes and her jaw drops as she stares at me.

"You…you can't be serious…"

"I'm very serious," I assure her. "Look, my relationship with my parents is…complicated. They want me to get married and live the life they've planned for me, but I'm not interested in that at all. I don't want to really get married, but I need to get out from under my dad's thumb."

"So, to get away from your dad, you want to go on a low budget tour with a total stranger?"

Grinning, I nod. "I know, it sounds wild, but how about I sweeten the pot? I'll fund the entire trip. All you have to do is pretend to be my fiance, otherwise you go about your life as you've planned. I don't want to get in the way of your goals for this trip."

Arya places her hands on her hips and just stares at me for several long moments. I hold her gaze, trying to silently convince her that I'm not kidding and will do everything I've said if she agrees to go along with my plan.

"This is crazy," she murmurs at length.

"Yeah, it is, but what do you have to lose?"

"We don't even know each other." She shakes her head. "How do I know whether or not you're a massive asshole?"

Grinning, I shrug. "Guess you'll just have to take that risk, huh?"

She tilts her head and her expression turns contemplative. Taking me seriously at last? I hold my breath, waiting for her to give me her answer...

The door to my room flies open and my father comes storming back inside. Arya jumps in surprise and moves closer to me. Whether she's looking to protect me or hoping for protection, I'm not certain, but I'm very pleased with the move.

My dad comes to a stop next to my bed and glares between the two of us. Mom isn't with him this time. I imagine she grew frustrated with his temper and left the hospital without him. It wouldn't be the first time such a scenario had played out—her anger with him and concern for how a public scene might make her look is more pressing than comforting her injured son.

I wish I could say I was surprised.

"All right," my dad spits. "If you're so bold that you'd get engaged without consulting your family, then you don't need to wait, do you?"

"What do you mean, Dad?" I growl, my body tensing as if anticipating a physical blow.

"Judge Anderson owes me a favor," he declares. "He's available tomorrow and I've arranged for him to officiate a civil ceremony for you two."

Son of a bitch. I know Judge Anderson—he's one of Dad's golfing buddies. I'm not surprised he'd so willingly offer to conduct a ceremony on such short notice. Dad has contributed generously to his election campaigns in the past.

I look up at Arya, and the color has drained from her face.

She blinks down at me, her mouth opening and closing on whatever denial she can't seem to get out.

"Or," my dad continues, his tone turning smug, "perhaps you'd like to back out, Ethan? Admit that this whole thing was a stupid mistake and pretend it never happened?"

Clenching my jaw, I narrow my eyes as I turn my gaze up to his. He's smirking, looking triumphant...so certain that he's winning this argument and yanking me into line. Well, he's dead wrong. If there's one thing my father has taught me that's actually stuck, it's not to back down from a challenge.

Forcing myself to relax into my pillows as I put on an air of nonchalance, I offer my dad a challenging smile and shake my head.

"You don't have to worry about that, Dad," I assure him.

His face falls in a second and he looks stunned before he catches himself and regains control of his reactions.

"You're making a mistake," he snarls.

Reaching up, I take hold of Arya's hand and pull it to my lips, giving her fingers a brief kiss that makes her gasp.

All the while, I hold my dad's glare, refusing to turn away from him.

"Don't you worry," I assure him, "I've never been more certain of anything in my entire life."

Clearly furious, Dad turns and storms out of the room once more, and watching him go feels like a victory.

———

"Explain this to me again. You're marrying this complete stranger as a fuck-you to Dad?"

Sitting back in my chair I look up from the glass of scotch in my hand to my brother, Jesse. It's the night before my 'wedding,' and he insisted on us going out to his favorite bar for drinks.

A kind of bachelor party, I suppose.

This isn't the kind of place I usually enjoy. It's too…rich. Sleek, modern, and exclusive with VIP areas, old men in suits smoking Cubans, and top-shelf booze that costs more per glass than a full meal for most people.

All right, I'll be honest…I don't mind the pricey booze.

Still, I don't fit in here. Jesse is wearing a gray suit with shiny black shoes and a slicked back haircut that I've told him more than once makes him look like a prick. In contrast, I'm wearing ripped jeans, a black t-shirt, and scuffed combat boots. My hair is too long and shaggy, and my jaw is covered in stubble. I'm uncomfortable and on edge, but Jesse is the only one of my siblings that I'm actually close to.

He's the only one who doesn't judge me for not fitting the Cavenwell mold, so I can put up with this place for one evening for him.

"Not only that," I reply with a smirk. "Though that's definitely a plus."

"Okay," Jesse sighs in exasperation. "What are the other reasons?"

"The trust fund," I say. "If I get married, I finally get my money. There's nothing in the agreement that says I have to marry someone Dad chooses. I just have to be married."

Jesse arches a brow. "So you're using this girl to get your money."

Chuckling, I reply, "you make me sound like such a cold bastard."

"Isn't that your whole thing?"

I roll my eyes. "She's getting something out of this too. She's a musician—I'm going to bankroll her tour. She'll be well compensated for her services."

Jesse barks out a humorless laugh. "'Services?' Holy shit, Ethan. You're such an asshole."

"I'm just doing what I have to so I can get free of all this bullshit," I grumble.

"Then what?" Jesse asks. "You marry this girl, you get your

trust, you're 'free,' whatever the fuck that means; What are you going to do with yourself after all that?"

I sit back and gaze at my brother, reluctant to answer because...I don't know what I'll do then. I've spent my whole life rebelling against my father, fighting to get away from his rules and demands that I haven't really had time to think about what I'll do beyond that. I just need to get away, and then I'll figure it out. One step at a time. Once I have my money, I'll be able to do whatever I want.

I'll worry about the rest then.

"I'm figuring it out," I tell Jesse. "First thing's first...I need to get my money."

"Well, cheers, brother," Jesse says, raising his glass to me. "To you and your blushing bride."

Even though I know he's being sarcastic, I lift my glass and clink it against his. To my blushing bride, and everything she's going to bring me.

"LADY, you either have to get off the bus or stay on. You can't just stand in the doorway."

Gasping, I look over my shoulder at the bus driver who's glaring at me in clear irritation.

"Oh, sorry." I quickly step off the bus onto the sidewalk. He shuts the door behind me and drives off, leaving me alone standing in front of the courthouse. The afternoon sun beats down on me, causing beads of sweat to instantly break out across my forehead. Crap, am I really doing this? I'm wearing a short white dress I bought at a thrift store, all my worldly possessions are in a giant worn suitcase at my side, along with my two violin cases. I'm not exactly the blushing bride I always imagined I'd be on my wedding day, but I also had never imagined that I'd be marrying a total stranger in exchange for one hundred thousand dollars.

Still, my life is changing today whether I get married or not. I gave up my tiny apartment, so it's tour time or bust. It'll just be a matter of if I'm going by myself or bringing Ethan along with me.

Honestly, I'm having some serious regret about agreeing to this. It was such a reckless, half-baked thing to jump on board with. However, I can't just ignore the money Ethan's offering. It's not that I'm looking for a handout or charity, but I can't just pretend that's not life-changing money that would go a long way in helping me achieve my dream. Still, I'm torn up inside with guilt, thinking about how this is a kind of betrayal to my brother.

Lou raised me until I was sixteen, and then everything fell apart because he was in the wrong place at the wrong time. He was walking home through a rich area of town after dark because his car broke down and he missed the bus. He just happened to be nearby right after the Cavenwells had been robbed.

My brother obviously had nothing to do with it, but Jared Cavenwell had the police arrest him because he looked 'suspicious,' *AKA not wearing designer clothes*. The investigation was closed in maybe five minutes—Cavenwell had so much clout with the police they didn't bother looking for another suspect.

I want to destroy Ethan's dad for framing my brother, and that's only one of the reasons I shouldn't go through with this. I did a Google search of my "fiance," and what I found was... unnerving. Ethan is apparently the rebel of the family, as well as being the youngest. He's gotten into a lot of trouble over the years, and not just the bored rich boy type of trouble. Like real, dangerous trouble. Fights that have landed people in the hospital, for instance.

It seems Ethan Cavenwell has a bit of a mean streak.

Am I really going to marry this man? *How can I say no when the payout is so high?*

Sucking in a deep breath, I lift my chin and start climbing the cement steps up to the court house's entrance.

Stepping into the lobby with its marble floors and high-arched ceiling, I immediately spot Ethan and my misgivings only intensify. He's wearing a black suit, crisp white shirt, and black tie. He looks so handsome, my heart starts to race.

Unfortunately, he's not alone. His parents are standing with him, and another man who bears a striking resemblance. He has to be a brother or some close relative like that.

They all turn and look at me, and while Ethan's gaze is welcoming, his parents are certainly not looking at me that way. They're glaring at me and are clearly disappointed that I've shown up. The other man is just watching me curiously. Facing down their intense stares, I feel a cold sweat start to break out along my forehead and down my neck.

Something in my expression must give away what's going through my head right now because Ethan furrows his brow in concern and makes his way over to me.

"Hey," he murmurs, laying a hand gently on my shoulder. "Are you all right?"

My breathing is coming in short pants and I shake my head.

"No…no, I'm not okay. I don't think I can do this after all, Ethan."

"Hey, hey, hey," he quickly says, looking around as if to make sure no one heard me. "It's okay. Come this way for a second."

Grabbing my suitcase and violins from me, he sets them at the security desk. A moment later he slips his hand to the small of my back and guides me toward a cracked door to our right. We slip inside and he shuts the door behind me. It's quiet in here and full of filing cabinets. It's some storage room, apparently. Ethan gazes down at me, his brow furrowed, angling his body to block the door while not crowding me, as if he knows that would just freak me out more.

"What's going on?" he asks, searching my face. "You looked terrified out there."

The scent of his spicy cologne teases my nose. Warmth unfurls in my belly and begins to slowly spread throughout me.

"I…I am terrified," I admit in a whisper. "Your parents—this is a really bad idea."

"No, it's not," he insists. "I know this is a lot, but just remember what you're gaining."

I release a long breath. "The hundred thousand is very generous, but…"

"Not just that. Remember that I'm going to pay for the entire tour as well."

That's true…I'd kind of let that detail of his offer slip from my mind. There are so many bookings on my trip that aren't fully paid for yet. My plan had been to pay as I went, using whatever profits I earned from one gig to pay for another. Far from a perfect plan, I know, but a workable one if I'm careful with my money.

However, having all of that taken care of and not having to worry? That would be such a weight lifted off my shoulders. I'd be able to focus completely on my music and I wouldn't have to stress about whether I could afford my next gig.

Gazing up at Ethan, I whisper, "you're really going to cover my whole tour?"

"I am," he replies.

"It seems almost too good to be true."

"I understand, but remember, I'm getting something out of this too. I'm not doing this purely out of the generosity or the goodness of my heart. Give it a shot, Arya. If, by the end of the tour, you really can't stand me, we'll get an amicable divorce and part ways. How's that sound?

That makes me feel somewhat at ease, and his reminder that this isn't just a handout but a mutually beneficial arrangement and we're both getting something out of this lessens some of my guilt. I'm doing this in part for my career, and in part for Lou. If my tour is a success and I can establish myself, I can use my newly earned money and influence to try and find my brother.

We can be a family again.

Ethan regards me closely. My breath leaves me in a rush as I stare up into his hypnotic blue eyes. He really is the most beautiful man I've ever met. Heat unfurls within my belly and spreads throughout my body, making my fingers and toes tingle. His fingers skim along my cheek, making me shiver.

"Okay," I whisper. "I'll do it."

My answer appears to please him. He gives me a half grin and leans closer to me. I gasp when his lips press against mine in a sudden kiss. His hand cups the back of my head and he deepens the kiss, tracing his tongue along the seam of my lips. I part them instinctively and he slips his tongue into my mouth. The heat that's burning through me gets hotter and hotter, until it feels as though my blood sizzles. Sliding my hands up his chest, I curl my fingers into his shirt and cling to him. His kiss is lulling me into a lust-filled daze and I can't seem to find the strength to break out of it.

I'm not really sure I want to.

Ethan is the one to break the kiss in the end. He stops and slowly pulls back, grinning down at me as I stare up at him, totally dumbfounded.

"Wh…what was that for?" I stammer.

"I didn't want our first kiss to be in front of those vultures," he explains.

That's oddly sweet…I think. He's got me totally turned upside down right now. I'm struggling to have any truly coherent thoughts as I continue to gaze up at him.

"Come on," he says with a grin, taking hold of my hand. "I think we've kept them waiting long enough. Let's go."

He turns and leads me out of the storage room. His family is still waiting for us in the lobby and as we approach, his mother gives me a withering look.

"You've wasted quite enough of our time," she snaps. "Are we going through with this ridiculous farce or not?"

Ethan glares at his mother. "Yes, we are going through with the wedding, so let's go find Judge Andersen."

He doesn't wait for any of them to reply and continues forward, his hand still firmly clasped around mine.

———

After signing a prenup that his parents insist upon—stating if we divorce, I'll leave with the assets I brought into the marriage and will have no claim on his money—we finally start our wedding. The ceremony is short and to the point. Ethan and I exchange vows that are rather basic and promise to love and cherish each other until death do us part. There's a moment where I'm glad we're not doing this in a church. I'd feel a lot guiltier lying in a church.

The whole time, I can feel his parents' disapproval practically radiating off of them. His brother, Jesse, who I'm hastily introduced to, stands off to the side and watches with a small grin playing about his lips. I still can't tell if he approves of this marriage or not. He's hard to read, and I'm usually good at reading people.

When we get to the ring exchange, I'm not really expecting Ethan to present me with anything more than a simple band, if that, but he surprises me when he slides a velvet box from his pocket. He opens it to reveal a gorgeous diamond ring that looks like an antique. The gold band is warm and slightly worn, and a delicate floral motif etched into the gold is still visible despite its age.

The center stone catches the light just so—a modest diamond with a subtle sparkle that feels both precious and understated. Smaller diamonds are set around the main stone, their sparkle like distant stars, adding a touch of glamor without overwhelming the ring's timeless charm.

Taking my hand, he puts it on my finger. I stare down at it, mesmerized by the diamond and the way it shimmers when the light catches it. The more I look at it, the more familiar it seems. It's so strange, and I look up at Ethan with a confused, furrowed brow. He's looking at Judge Andersen, waiting for the ceremony to continue.

I take a deep breath and push those strange feelings aside. My head is in a weird place, that's all. Overthinking and over-analyzing. Looking for any sign that this isn't right because I'm paranoid, that's all. I turn my attention to the judge as he begins wrapping up the ceremony.

"By the power vested in me by the state of Texas," Judge Andersen declares. "I now pronounce you husband and wife. You may kiss the bride."

Just like that, I'm married. Ethan turns back to me and, without a word, leans down to press a quick kiss to my lips. It's completely different from the passionate one we shared not long ago in the supply room. There's no warmth in this brief exchange. He's all business right now, which I suppose I can understand, given how tense the atmosphere around us is.

Turning to his family, he gives his father a brief, hard hand-shake. No words of congratulations are exchanged. No warm wishes.

His mother glares at me as he moves to his brother to shake his hand as well. The two do share a quick exchange that I can't hear, and then Ethan turns and quickly makes his way to me. He takes my hand again and squeezes it.

"Are you ready to go?" he asks.

That's a more loaded question than I think he realizes. Ready to go? Ready to start on this strange new life I've somehow tumbled into? Ready to spend the next few weeks with a man who doesn't even know who I really am?

I'm a Cavenwell now…Lou would be so disgusted with me.

I remind myself that I'm doing this in part for him. If I can make this tour a success and jumpstart my career, I can then try to find my brother and reunite with him. We'll be a family again.

Gazing up at Ethan, I nod. This is the best chance I have to finally get everything I've been dreaming of since I was sixteen.

"Yes," I tell him. "I'm ready."

Without another word, he makes his way to the door leading out of the judge's chambers, pulling me along behind him.

It doesn't strike me until this moment that I'm rushing off to my wedding night with my new husband. What is he going to expect? Will he want sex?

Do I want sex?

I haven't really considered what comes after the wedding, but now, it's all I can think about...and I'm not exactly sure how I want this night to end.

Chapter Five

ETHAN

MOM SURPRISED me by booking Arya and I a room in The Luxe, a five-star hotel, for our wedding night. I'm not sure what to make of that, other than she's likely trying to avoid causing any rumors by not showing some type of support for my marriage. Whatever her motivation, it's a gesture that I can tell Arya appreciates. Upon walking into the lavish room, she gazes around with wide-eyes, clearly in awe. I stand back and watch as she explores the large room and massive bathroom. She tests the couch and chairs in a seating area next to a floor-to-ceiling window, opens the doors of the armoire, inspects the minibar, and hops up onto the king-sized bed to lie in the pile of pillows.

"Wow," she says, a wide grin spreading across her face. "A girl could get used to this."

I chuckle and shake my head. "Soak it up and enjoy. It's been a long day, so get some rest."

She sits up and gazes at me with those bright blue eyes of hers. "I'm not sure I can rest right now. I'm too wired. So much has happened."

That's the understatement of the century. Seeing how frustrated my parents were throughout our wedding was a small but sweet victory. For years, I've felt trapped by their expectations and their relentless grip on my life and choices. Marrying Arya was my way of breaking free, not just from their control but from the life they've had meticulously planned for me since I was a kid.

The look of helplessness on their faces, knowing they could no longer dictate my actions, was deeply satisfying. Today was a turning point for me and I'm not going back to my life before this, no matter what my parents try to do to lure me home.

"Yeah," I agree with a long breath. "A lot has fucking happened."

"Your parents were clearly furious," she continues. "But your brother didn't seem that upset about our marriage."

Of my four siblings, I'm closest to Jessie. We're also closest in age, with him only being two years older than me at twenty-seven. My other siblings are all in their thirties and married. I don't have much in common with them, and they don't have that much time for me now that they've all got their own families.

"He understands how difficult things between me and my parents are," I confess. "He supports me trying to get away from their control."

She winces at that. "I see. At least they showed up and stuck around, unlike at the hospital. That reminds me, how are you feeling?"

I arch a brow at her. "Playing the concerned wife now?"

"You did get hurt because of me," she says. "And since I am your wife, I do have some responsibility to make sure you are whole and healthy, don't I? I'm not sure…I didn't have time to read the happy-wife handbook."

"I'm fine," I assure her. "You don't have to worry."

She doesn't look convinced, and in truth, I've had some killer headaches since waking up in the hospital, but the doctor assured me those would go away in time. I don't need to be taken care of, so I don't share that bit of information with her.

"If there's anything I can do to help you," she says, "please let me know. I owe you."

I chuckle at that and shake my head. "You agreed to lie to my family and marry me. I think we're more than even."

My phone buzzes in my pocket. I dig it out and scowl when I see that my dad is texting me. Shit, what does he want? Hasn't he ripped into me enough for the day?

I open the first message and sigh. Apparently not.

> I've never been so disappointed in you, Ethan. I put up with your lack of interest in the company for years because I expected you'd shape up and realize that you need to step up for this family, but clearly I was wrong.

That's not the only text message he's sent me.

> Marrying this nobody just to spite me? Did you really think I wouldn't see right through you? You're not nearly as clever as you think you are.

> You've spit in the face of every opportunity I've given you. You haven't attended a single one of my political rallies and it's an election year, nor have you attended any board meetings for the Cavenwell conglomerate. I gave you that position in the finance department at the law firm, and you pissed it away by not showing up and half-assing the work. You are wasting your life and your talents!

> Mark my words, you're going to regret marrying that little slut.

That last text has my temper really flaring. He's still trying to assert control of me, even though I've met his stipulation that I marry. Sure, Arya isn't who he would've wanted me to marry, but he can't deny that I've met my requirement to gain access to my trust fund and break free from my family's hold.

Gritting my teeth, I drop my phone before I crush it.

"You okay?" Arya asks, frowning in concern.

"Fine," I growl. "Just fine."

Except I'm not fine. Not at all. My dad has a talent for pissing me off with having to try very hard. I need to be alone right now so I can get my temper under control. I don't want Arya to see just how much my father affects me. It's damn humiliating, but just makes me that much more determined to get out from under his thumb.

"Ethan?" Arya calls out. She's on her hands and knees, grabbing a menu from the bedside table. "Do you want anything from room service?"

I'm only half-listening and shake my head as I grunt and make my way into the bathroom, shutting the door behind me. Maybe a shower will help cool me off. I don't want to deal with my dad and his bullshit right now. He can keep texting me all he wants to tell me how much of a disappointment I am...I just won't respond.

Once I have control of my trust fund, he won't have anything else to hold over me.

Stripping off my clothes, I turn the hot water on and step under the stream, releasing a long sigh as I run my hands through my hair. Thinking back on the day, I feel a rush of frustration thinking of my family. They just can't let go. No matter what I do, they refuse to release their choke hold on me, especially my father.

I will say that it was very satisfying seeing how shocked everyone was when I gave Arya my grandmother's ring. I'd swiped it from Mom and Dad's house yesterday. They'd been withholding it, always claiming that one of my married brothers would get it, but never deciding who. So, since no one else has had the chance to use it, I took it myself. I knew it would piss off my parents and be the ultimate 'fuck-you' to them and their plans for me.

What I'm serious about is getting access to my trust fund so I can live the life I want with no more monkey suits or smiling constituents. My dad's political ambitions are of no interest to me, but so long as he refuses to hand over my trust fund, he's got me on a leash. Under the spray of the hot shower, I start to relax and am able to think more clearly. My marriage is a condition I have to meet to access the trust—it's in writing. No matter how much my dad might protest, I'm legally allowed to get that money.

I can get the paperwork in place to request the funds, and he'll no doubt try to stop me, he doesn't have a legal foot to stand on. That helps calm me down further. Finishing up my shower, I turn off the water and step out on the bathroom floor mat. I pause and look around, only now remembering that I left my suitcase out in the main room.

Shit. Not much choice but to go out there half-naked. Hopefully, I don't scandalize my new fake wife.

Grabbing a towel, I wrap it around my waist and open the bathroom door. Immediately, the soft music of Arya's violin wraps around me and I pause in my tracks. She's sitting cross-legged on the bed, her back to me, and her violin tucked under her chin. Though it's electric, she doesn't have it plugged in. She's playing it with an ease that's kind of enchanting to watch.

She doesn't appear to notice that I've come back in the room, she's so engrossed in her playing.

I haven't been able to really appreciate how pretty she is until this moment. She's still wearing her wedding dress, but she's kicked off her shoes and is barefoot and more visibly relaxed than she was at any point in the courthouse. Thinking about our conversation in the storage room, I realize how close she'd been to backing out of our plan. She'd been scared, I'd seen it in her big blue eyes. The way she'd been looking at me made me question whether she was hesitant to marry in general, or hesitant to specifically marry *me*. The thought had left me strangely anxious. A sense of desperation had overtaken me and I'd kissed her as a way to try and calm her down and keep her from running, but it had quickly gotten hotter than I'd anticipated.

Her lips were soft, and the way she'd pressed her curvy body against me had turned me on and made me want to explore every inch of her. The fact that she'd so eagerly accepted my kiss had stirred something deep inside me that I hadn't anticipated.

Swallowing, I snap myself out of those thoughts and focus back on her sitting on the bed. I need to keep it together. I'm not against a dirty, hot fuck, but that would only complicate things between us and I need to keep my eye on the prize. Arya is my ticket to freedom, and I'm not going to risk this opportunity just to get my dick wet. We hadn't discussed sex or anything like that, and it hadn't been the highest priority in my head when I'd thought through this scheme. Now, it's hitting me that I have a very beautiful wife sitting in the middle of the bed on our wedding night.

What man could resist such an opportunity?

She stops playing and reaches over the bedside table to pick up a flute of champagne. Champagne? I see she's not wasting any time indulging in the good life.

I take a step forward, determined to shut down her little party before she gets the wrong idea about our stay here, but then she puts down her champagne and picks her violin back up. As she begins to play again, I can't help but stop and listen to her again. This time, her music is more classical. More sensual. Not at all what I'd have expected given her overly sunny demeanor and the country rock she was playing at the bar the other night.

Huh, that's interesting. It seems there are several more layers to my blushing bride than I thought.

How…intriguing. I'm suddenly overwhelmed with the idea

of unwrapping each and every one of her layers to see what surprises she has hiding underneath.

RICH CHOCOLATE and fresh strawberries fill the air as I take another sip of champagne, the bubbles dancing on my tongue. I can't help but smile as I look at the spread of room service on the bedside table—indulgent, extravagant, and completely unnecessary. And yet, here I am, savoring every bite, every sip, and loving the recklessness of it all. Life, as it were, offered me champagne, and I decided to take it.

The events of the day swirl in my mind like the fizz in my glass. I'm married. To a man I barely know. The logical part of my brain is screaming at me to be careful and to stay on guard, but here I am, alone in a hotel room with Ethan, my husband. The truth is, I'm curious. There's something about him that I can't ignore—a mystery that I find oddly compelling and am rather eager to unravel.

The champagne isn't helping. It's only fueling the fire, making me feel bold. I lean against the plush pillows along the bed's headboard, letting the bubbles work their magic, and my eyes drift to the violin case I brought with me. I reach for it, my fingers almost itching to play. Shifting to the middle of the bed, I cross my legs and carefully take out the violin and settle it under my chin. My fingers find the strings, and I start plucking away. The notes are soft, tentative, but as they fill the room, they start to take shape. The sound is soothing, grounding me in a way that nothing else can. Each pluck of the string resonates in the silence, a gentle reminder that I'm doing what I need to in order to make my dreams come true. This marriage, this tour… it's all for my music in the end.

As I play, I let my thoughts drift back to Ethan. He's a much more complicated man than I would have guessed. Being a Cavenwell, I'd have assumed he was selfish, snobbish, and cared only for his image and reputation. However, after seeing the way he interacted with his family—the tension and coolness, especially between him and his father—I can't help but wonder if he's anything like the rest of his family. He doesn't match the Cavenwell image I have in my head, and if he's different from the others, maybe he didn't have any hand in what happened to my brother. That thought causes a flutter in my chest that feels very much like hope.

Maybe I haven't betrayed my brother after all.

There's something almost surreal about being married to someone like him—a man who's clearly used to getting what he wants, who moves through life with a confidence that's both intimidating and intriguing. I don't know what to make of him yet, but I can't deny that there's an attraction there, a spark that I wasn't expecting. He's just so damn sexy. I've never met a man as attractive as Ethan…not in real life anyway. He's so tall and dark and…ripped. God, whenever I look at him, I have to fight to not stare. His shirts cling to his bulging arms and his wide chest, and a part of me wants so badly to see exactly what's underneath and run my fingers along every bump and crevice of his torso. Then, slowly work my way lower and lower until…

A floorboard squeaks behind me, yanking me out of my thoughts. The sound is subtle, yet it sends a shiver down my spine, and I realize the water running in the shower has stopped. My heart skips a beat and my cheeks flush with guilt and embarrassment as I lower my violin and turn around to find Ethan standing in the doorway wearing nothing but a towel.

Holy shit…he's even more chiseled and gorgeous than I anticipated. Water droplets still cling to his skin, sliding down the contours of his broad, muscular chest. His dark hair, damp and tousled from the shower, gives him an effortless, rugged look, as if he'd just stepped out of a magazine shoot rather than a bathroom.

He steps into the room, and as he moves, the muscles in his arms and shoulders ripple. There's something magnetic about the way he carries himself—confident, powerful, and utterly unbothered by the fact that he's nearly naked in front of me.

The sight is enough to make me catch my breath, and I can feel my cheeks warming under his gaze, especially when his eyes drift over my body like a touch.

He raises an eyebrow. "I didn't realize you were having a party without inviting me."

His voice is smooth, laced with just enough teasing to make my pulse quicken. I can't help but smile, feeling mischievous. I've been riding this high all evening, and right now, I'm not in the mood to let it fade.

I give him a playful look. "I didn't realize I had an audience."

His eyes flash like I've issued a challenge he can't refuse and a grin quirks the corner of his lips. I pop another strawberry into my mouth and stick my tongue out at him, holding the berry there with a grin. Ethan's eyes narrow slightly, but there's a glint of amusement in them. He takes a step closer, and damn if it doesn't look like his towel is barely holding on.

*If it just slips a little lower…*my thighs press together instinctively as I feel myself grow wet. My eyes drop to the V below his waist.

"Is that so?" he says, his voice low, almost a growl.

Before I can say anything in response, he reaches the side of the bed and leans down toward me. Stunned, I freeze as he brings his mouth close to mine and snatches the strawberry from my mouth with his teeth. My heart squeezes and a rush of arousal shoots straight to my core.

He doesn't back away as he slowly chews the strawberry and keeps his gaze locked on mine.

"Ethan..." His name is a breathless whisper that dissolves into a gasp of surprise when he closes the distance between us and kisses me.

It's whisper soft, his lips skimming mine, and the touch is electric. His second kiss is firmer, more demanding, and when his tongue sweeps into my mouth I'm overwhelmed by the taste of him. More. I need more. I thread my fingers through his hair and pull him tighter to me as he devours my mouth.

Time ceases to matter as we fall onto the bed together. His hands move from holding my face down my sides until he's gripping my hips. He grinds himself against me and I let my legs fall open in clear invitation. I don't even care that we probably shouldn't be doing this because it only complicates an already crazy situation further. It just feels so good that I can't find it in me to put a stop to it.

The room feels smaller, more intimate, the soft lighting casting shadows that seem to dance around us. His mouth is warm, soft, but there's an undeniable hunger in the way he kisses me. My hands slide up to his chest, fingers splayed against his firm, bare skin. I can feel the muscles tense under my touch, and it sends a shiver down my spine.

His tongue teases the edge of my bottom lip, and I open up to him, letting him in, the taste of him dizzying. My hands tangle in his hair, pulling him even closer as the kiss grows hotter, more intense. His other hand slides up my side, his touch firm but gentle, and my heart threatens to leap out of my chest.

Ethan is the one to break our kiss and as he's holding my gaze, he moves down my body, presses kisses against me through the barrier of my dress. It doesn't fully register what he's doing until he moves my legs to rest over his shoulders.

Holy shit! Is he…?

Smirking, he slips my panties down my legs, maneuvering them to pull the tiny bit of lace off me before tossing it away to land somewhere on the floor. When he lowers his head to my pussy, my whole body shudders. The first swipe of his tongue sends a jolt of pleasure shooting through me, like I'm getting struck by lightning. His hands wrap around my thighs, gripping me tight and holding me down as I undulate against him. The feel of his fingers pressing into my skin is a delicious contrast to the warmth and delicate touch of his tongue. He continues, licking and kissing, it's like I'm losing my mind, but I don't want him to stop. This feels so good…almost too good… like a hit of something strong and addictive.

"Oh, my God," I groan when his lips wrap around my clit. When he starts to suck, I nearly jerk off the bed as stars explode in my vision. My hands find the top of his head and I tangle my fingers in his hair. I don't want him to even try to get away from me before he makes me come. He slips one finger inside me and I throw my head bag and let out a desperate cry.

When his tongue presses against my clit, I nearly lose my mind. I tighten my grip on his hair and he groans against me. His fingers press into my thighs so hard, I know he's going to leave bruises, but I don't care. I just need him to keep going.

"Don't stop," I hiss. "Don't you dare stop!"

He does just the opposite, lifting his head to snap, "you think you're the boss right now?"

"What?" I gasp, gazing down at him. "What the hell are you talking about?"

He twists the finger inside of me, making me whimper.

"Who's in charge?" he demands, pumping his finger in and out of me harder.

What game is he playing right now? I'm wound up so tight

that I'll do or say just about anything to make sure he gets me off.

"You," I manage to declare in a breathless voice. "You're in charge, Ethan."

"So you come when I say you come."

"Yes, please…please let me…"

He growls and starts licking and sucking with more force and I'm teetering on the edge within moments.

"Come," he demands. "Right now."

He put his mouth back on me and that's all I need.

"Ethan!" I cry when my orgasm explodes through me. My body is no longer my own as I jerk and writhe, lost to the intense pleasure of my release.

Ethan doesn't let up until he's wrung every last bit of my orgasm out of me. He finally lifts his head with a cocky grin when I'm a boneless puddle in the middle of the bed, fighting to catch my breath.

Glancing down, my eyes land on the prominent bulge in his towel. Licking my lips, I imagine taking him deep into my mouth and giving him the pleasure he just gave me, but before I can reach out to pull him back, he tightens the towel around his waist and moves away from the bed.

"Wait…where are you going?"

He glances at me, and his expression is hard to read. "This was just for you. Call it a wedding present…to help you relax and relieve some stress."

I stare at him, stunned. "But, don't you…need relief too?"

Giving me a small smirk, he shakes his head. "No, I'm all right. I don't want to overwhelm you or make you feel pressured. It's been a long day. I'm going to get dressed and you should get some rest. We've got a busy six months ahead of us"

Before I can say another word, he grabs his suitcase and heads into the bathroom, shutting the door behind him.

Wait…what? Is that it?

Blinking, I rest against the bed and stare up at the ceiling in stunned silence. My heart hammers in my chest and my mind is still hazy with pleasure. I never thought a Cavenwell would make me feel like this…pleasured, satisfied, and desired. Then, to not expect anything in return? It's not at all what I would have expected.

What are the next six months of this arrangement going to be like…and what will it cost me when I get my regular life back in the end?

Chapter Seven

ETHAN

THE EARLY MORNING light filters through the haze, casting a soft, golden glow over the empty parking lot as we step out of the hotel. The air is cool, with a faint crispness that hints at the start of fall. Arya walks ahead of me, her hair catching the light as it sways gently with each step.

The car is parked close by, a few spaces from the entrance. It's a sleek, black Mercedes Benz sedan. I pop the trunk, the faint clink of metal breaking the silence as I move to grab the luggage from the cart. The wheels squeak as I pull it closer, and the thud of the suitcase hitting the ground seems to echo in the quiet morning.

Shifting our suitcases around in the trunk, I finally manage to get everything packed into the car and shut it with a deep sigh. I turn toward Arya, who's standing beside the car. Her head is down and she appears lost in thought. I watch her, my mind wandering to last night. I'm still not sure what came over me when I pushed her onto the bed and licked her sweet pussy. I really hadn't done it expecting anything in return, but when she offered, I was beyond tempted. Yet, I resisted. I'm still not sure how I managed to walk away from her, but I forced myself to. I may be a bastard, especially in my family's eyes, but I'm not a monster. I wasn't going to take advantage of Arya after the emotionally charged and confusing day we had together. She still doesn't really know me, and if she did, she'd likely have thought twice about agreeing to marry me. I need to be careful with her. We're only together for six months or so while she's on tour, and I need to maintain control of myself and stay focused on my plan.

"Are you ready?" I ask.

Seemingly startled at my addressing her, she looks up at me, her eyes widening.

"Oh, yeah, I am. Sorry…spaced out there."

I can only imagine what's going through her head. Neither of us have mentioned what happened last night. It's as if we're both trying to pretend it was a fluke. Not something to be repeated. Maybe if we ignore it, we can also ignore the tension and heat that seems to be sizzling between us since we've met.

"Let's get going, then." To be a gentleman, I open the car door for her. She gives me an arched brow look and then slides into the front seat. Closing the door behind her, I move around to the driver's side and get in behind the wheel. She's quiet as I start the car and pull away from the hotel.

It isn't long before the silence feels suffocating, and I don't want to just sit here letting my thoughts run wild and my memories of what she tasted like and how she responded to my touch completely take over.

"So," I begin after clearing my throat as I shift in my seat, trying to sound casual. "This tour…seems like a pretty big deal for you." My voice comes out rougher than I intend, betraying the curiosity—and maybe something else—buzzing beneath the surface.

Arya turns to look at me, her eyes lighting up, and it's like the tiredness from the morning fades away in an instant. "Yeah, it's a huge deal. This is what's going to jumpstart my music career, and when I get to New York, I'll hopefully have enough clout built up that I can get signed by a record label."

I nod, trying to keep my tone even. "I see. That makes sense. You're planning on staying in New York?"

She shrugs, but there's a hopeful gleam in her eyes. "That's the plan. New York's where everything happens, right? I mean, if I'm serious about making a name for myself, that's where I need to be."

I lean back, letting her words sink in.

"What about your place here? You have an apartment? Or… wherever you live?" The question comes out awkward, but I'm curious. Wondering what happens to the part of her that's here.

She bites her lip, looking thoughtful. "Yeah, I've got an apartment. I'll probably sublet it. Or maybe I'll just let it go. I don't know…it depends on how things pan out in New York."

"Sounds like you've got it all figured out."

She smiles, but there's something softer in it now. "I don't have everything figured out, Ethan. Just trying to make the most of this chance. But I'll be around…for now." Her eyes linger on me for a second longer before her gaze darts away.

"How'd you get started in music, anyway?"

The corner of her lips creep up into a small, wistful smile.

"I bounced from foster home to foster home between ages sixteen and eighteen, and the woman who ran the group home I finally ended up in taught me. Playing violin became an escape of sorts. When I was lonely or sad, I'd play my music and it'd make me feel better. Like I had some kind of control over my life. I've always tried to live with the mindset that even if things are tough, if I can change my attitude, I can make the situation better for me."

Releasing a snort, I murmur, "I usually prefer to just change the situation."

Arya's head turns slightly, and I catch the flicker in her eyes before she responds.

"Not everyone has the kind of power and influence you do,"

she says, her tone cooling. There's a sharp edge to her words, like she's trying to keep it casual but can't quite hide the bite.

"Sure." I shrug, pretending not to notice. "Still, I'm not the kind of guy that likes to leave things up to fate or others or whatever."

It's true. I've never been one to just sit back and wait for life to happen. I make my own choices, and I damn well make sure I control the outcome, but the way she's looking at me now, arms folded and eyes narrowing, I can tell she's not impressed.

"You don't say," she grumbles, sinking deeper into the seat like she's putting a wall up between us. Her gaze flicks to the window, and just like that, it feels like the temperature in the car has dropped a few degrees.

That was fast. Small talk is officially over.

I can feel the tension in her posture, the way her shoulders stiffen. What did I say? It's not like I'm lying. I don't play the waiting game, not with my life and definitely not with my business. Maybe she doesn't get that, or maybe...maybe she does, and that's the problem.

———

I'm speeding down the highway, which isn't unusual for me. I like the adrenaline rush I get when I'm dancing on the riskier side of life. Speeding gives me a small hit of that rush. We're halfway to Fort Smith when my stomach starts growling, the kind of deep, relentless hunger that makes it impossible to ignore. A roadside bar is a few miles up ahead. It looks like it's been here for decades—neon lights flickering, paint peeling off the sign, and a few bikes parked out front. It's not exactly the Ritz, but it'll do. I pull the car into the gravel lot, cutting the engine.

Arya looks at the bar, then back at me, her brow furrowing. "Are you serious? Here?" she asks, her voice tinged with disbelief.

"Yeah, here," I say, unclipping my seatbelt. "It's not five-star, but it's food."

"Do you ever eat anywhere that isn't five-star?" she scoffs.

I look at her and arch a brow. "I enjoy a cheap, greasy burger as much as the next guy."

She glances at the bar again, then at the parking lot. "Ethan, this place looks…well, it looks like the kind of place where cars like this disappear."

I stifle a sigh, already feeling my patience starting to wear thin. "It's fine, Arya. We're not in the middle of a crime scene. We'll be in and out."

Her concern doesn't fade; in fact, it deepens, her eyes narrowing as she crosses her arms. "But what about the car? And all my stuff? I don't want to leave everything out here in plain sight. Someone could break in."

I glance at her, trying to keep my tone even. "We'll park under a light. It'll be fine."

She's not convinced, and I can feel the tension starting to rise between us. "Ethan, I'm serious. This car is practically a beacon in a place like this. Can't we find somewhere else? Somewhere less…sketchy?"

Something inside me snaps, a mix of frustration and exasperation. I get that she's nervous, but I'm not about to drive another hour looking for a place that meets her standards.

"No, Arya. We're eating here. It's just a meal. We'll be out before you know it."

She shakes her head, her eyes flashing with defiance. "You're being reckless. You don't even care about my things, do you? My violins? They're my whole life! If I lose them, I'm fucked!"

I grit my teeth, trying to keep my temper in check, but it's getting harder by the second. "I care about getting food in my stomach and keeping us on schedule. If you want to sit here and worry, fine. I'm going in."

Before she can argue further, I grab the keys and get out of the car, slamming the door behind me. I hear her voice, sharp and insistent, but I'm already walking away, heading toward the bar. Space and distance are what I need from this pointless argument. I get that she's anxious, but I've been through worse places than this. It's nothing I can't handle.

Inside, I find a booth near the back of the bar where I can keep an eye on Arya through the window. The place is dimly lit, filled with the scent of grease and stale beer. It's not exactly the type of place I'd normally go to, but it suits my mood right now. I order a beer and some food, settling in with a clear view of the car and her still inside it, arms crossed. She looks pissed. Good, because I'm pissed too. Any minute, she'll realize I'm right and come slinking in here for food.

I take out my phone and dial Jesse. The phone rings a few times before he picks up, his voice casual and laced with amusement.

"Well, well, if it isn't the newlywed. How's married life treating you, Ethan?"

I take a swig of my beer, the cold liquid sliding down my throat as I glance out the window. "It's…more interesting than I expected."

My voice sounds casual, but my eyes are fixed on Arya, who's still sitting out there in the car. She's been out there for almost ten minutes now, stubborn as ever, and my irritation builds.

What is she doing? She could've come inside by now, but instead, she's just…lingering. Like she's trying to prove some point. Maybe she thinks I'll go out there and pull her in. That's not happening. I'm not playing into her little game. If she wants to sit in the car and sulk, fine. God, she's infuriating and stubborn as hell. She's driving me absolutely crazy.

I take another swig of my beer, trying to shake off the irritation, but it lingers.

At least she's not boring, and the way she moves her body

when she dances and the taste of her on my tongue…fuck, I'm getting distracted.

"I didn't call you to talk about that."

"Sure you didn't," Jesse chuckles. "You're not calling just to say hello, so what's up?"

"I need you to see about speeding up the trust fund transfer paperwork. I don't want to drag this out any longer than necessary."

There's a pause on the other end, and I can almost picture Jesse leaning back in his chair, his expression turning serious. "You know, Dad's saying this marriage won't last more than a month. He's dragging his feet on the money, says he won't give it up just yet."

I grip the beer bottle tighter, trying to keep my voice even. "Of course he is. I should've known he'd pull something like that."

"Look, I'll do what I can, but you know how he is. He's convinced this whole thing is just another one of your impulsive stunts. And Ethan…be careful with this girl."

I clench my jaw, a wave of anger rising in me. "I know what I'm doing, Jesse."

"I'm just saying, watch your back. I'll keep you posted on the paperwork."

I hang up, my anger simmering. I stare at my phone then toss it onto the table. I should've expected this, but it still pisses me off. My father's always trying to control everything, and Jesse's warning is just another reminder that nothing is ever as simple as it should be. I glance out the window, and that's when I see them—a couple of guys loitering near the car, their eyes fixed on Arya. One of them leans in, saying something to her through the window. She looks uncomfortable, her body tense.

Damn it.

I push back from the booth, scooping up the food and tossing some bills onto the counter. My steps quicken as I head toward the door, the anger I've been trying to keep in check flaring up again.

I don't know what those guys think they're doing, but they're about to find out just how bad of an idea it is to mess with my wife—even if this marriage is just a means to an end. As I push through the door and into the parking lot, Arya's eyes widen when she spots me, and the two guys turn to face me.

Time to handle the situation.

Chapter Eight

MY HEART POUNDS in my chest, the sound of it loud in my ears as the two guys lean closer to the car, their eyes hungry and predatory as they sweep over me. I try to keep my cool, flashing a smile through the open window that doesn't quite reach my eyes. Charm. That's always been my fallback. My shield when things get dicey. I've talked my way out of worse situations, but this…this is different. We're in the middle of nowhere, and these guys don't look like they're here for friendly conversation.

"Well, hello," one of the men says in a voice that makes my skin crawl. "What's a pretty thing like you doing out here by yourself?"

"Hey there," I say, my voice a little too bright, a little too shaky. "Just waiting for my husband. He'll be back any second."

They just exchange a glance, the taller one grinning like he knows a secret I don't. My pulse quickens, and I feel the edges of panic creeping in. I can't run, can't fight, so I keep talking, hoping to distract them.

"Nice night, isn't it?" My voice trembles despite my best efforts. "We're just passing through. I'm on tour. You guys from around here?"

The taller guy chuckles, stepping even closer to the car. "We're local, yeah, but I don't recognize you. I'd definitely remember a face like that if you were famous. What kind of tour are we talking about?"

My mouth is dry, my thoughts scattering as I try to keep the smile plastered on my face. "Music tour. I'm a musician."

"Oh, a musician," the other guy says, leaning on the car door. "Maybe you can play something for us. Right here, right now. Why don't you get on out of that car?"

I swallow hard, the panic clawing at me now. Where is Ethan? I glance around, praying he'll come out of the bar any second, but there's no sign of him.

"Sure, maybe later," I say, the words barely coming out. "But my husband really doesn't like it when I perform for strangers. You know how it is."

The tall guy's smile falters just a bit, but he doesn't back off. "Husband, huh? Where is he, then? What kind of man leaves his pretty young wife alone in a parking lot?"

I'm about to answer when I hear the bar door slam open, and suddenly, Ethan is there. Relief crashes over me so hard that I nearly sag in my seat. He strides over, his eyes cold and hard, and the two guys immediately straighten up, their cocky expressions fading.

"That's enough," Ethan says, his voice low and dangerous. "Get away from my wife."

Wife. The word hangs in the air, and everything is still. It's strange how…good that sounds. I'm not the type to usually ask for or accept help, but having Ethan standing there, calling me his wife and looking fierce and protective, makes me feel more willing to step back and let him handle this. The guys exchange a quick look, sizing up Ethan and clearly deciding he's not worth the trouble. They mutter something under their breaths and back off, walking away with a few backward glances. As soon as they're out of sight, Ethan's expression softens. He opens the car door, and I practically fall into his arms, the adrenaline and fear finally catching up to me. He holds me tight, his hand rubbing soothing circles on my back.

"I'm sorry," he murmurs, his voice close to my ear. "I shouldn't have left you alone like that."

I nod against his chest, too shaken to speak. His arms around me are solid, grounding, and I let myself lean into him, the panic slowly ebbing away. Then he pulls back just enough to look at me, a small, teasing smile tugging at the corner of his mouth.

"Hey, I brought you something," he says, holding up a burger and a bag of fries. "Better than whatever you're usually forced to eat on tour, right?"

"I wouldn't know, I've never been on tour before, but I appreciate the gesture. Still, I'm not hungry right now. I'll save it for later."

Grabbing the food from him, I open the car door with trembling hands and grab my acoustic violin's case. The weight of the case in my hand is familiar and comforting. I take a deep breath, trying to shake off the lingering fear from the close call. I need to calm down, to find my center again, and there's only one way I know how.

"Ethan," I say, my voice still a little shaky, "close your eyes for a minute."

He raises an eyebrow at me, clearly curious but obliges without question, his eyes fluttering shut. I carefully place the violin case on the hood of the car, my fingers finding the latch almost automatically. The case opens with a soft click, revealing my acoustic violin, its polished wood gleaming in the fading light.

There's a tiny, almost invisible slit in the lining of the violin case. I dig into the slit and fish out two emergency hundred-dollar bills from inside the violin. They're still there, thank God. Of course they would be, but with what just happened, feeling the paper between my fingertips puts me at ease. Being so close to losing everything I have is terrifying. As I tuck the bills in my pocket, I hear a soft chuckle. I spin around, and there's Ethan, eyes open, watching me with a smirk on his face.

"I thought I told you to close your eyes!" I say, crossing my arms in mock indignation.

"I did," he says, still smiling. "But then I got curious. I've never seen someone pull cash out of a violin before."

I can't help but laugh, the sound easing the tightness in my chest. "You weren't supposed to see that. It's my secret stash for emergencies. Not that I thought I'd ever actually need to use it, but…you know."

Ethan just shakes his head, his smile softening. "You're full of surprises, Arya."

My cheeks warm under his gaze, but I quickly turn to the violin, not ready to dwell on whatever that feeling is.

"Since you've seen that, how about I show you something else?" I suggest carefully lifting the violin out of its case. "I always say, you can't control everything, but you can control your attitude to improve the situation. With that in mind, I need to calm down, and this is the best way I know how."

He leans against the car, still watching me with that same curious expression. "What are you going to play?"

"You'll see," I say with a small smile. "Just…listen."

I tuck the violin under my chin and rest the bow lightly on the strings. I close my eyes, letting the cool evening air and the distant hum of traffic fade away. Then, with a deep breath, I draw the bow across the strings. The melody is one I've been working on for a while—it's a piece that's slowly taken shape over countless quiet moments like this one. It's soft and haunting, each note carefully chosen, a reflection of all the emotions I can't quite put into words. The music fills the space around us, wrapping us in its warmth as the sun dips below the horizon.

As I play, the tension leaves my body, the fear and anxiety

melting away with each note. The world narrows down to just the sound of the violin and the feather light weight of the bow in my hand. It's just me and the music. Nothing else matters.

I open my eyes, glancing at Ethan, and find him watching me with an intensity that makes my heart skip a beat. His burger, forgotten, sits untouched on the hood beside him as he listens, leaning back against the front of the car, completely absorbed in the music. There's something in his expression—something softer, almost vulnerable—that I've never seen before.

When I finish playing, the last note lingers in the air for several seconds before slowly fading into the night. I lower the violin, the bow trembling slightly in my hand as the silence settles between us. Neither of us speaks.

"That was..." Ethan starts, his voice low and rough, "incredible."

I give him a small, shy smile, my heart still fluttering in my chest. "Thanks. It's my way of...grounding myself, I guess."

He pushes off the car, stepping closer to me. There's something in his eyes that I can't quite read, but it makes my breath catch in my throat.

"You're really something, you know that?"

I bite my lip, feeling a flush of pleasure at the compliment. It's like he sees me for who I really am, and few ever have.

"Just doing what I love," I say softly.

His gaze is still locked on mine. "I think I'm starting to understand that."

The moment stretches out, the air between us charged with something unspoken. I'm not sure what to say, so I just carefully pack away the violin, closing the case with a quiet click.

Ethan clears his throat, breaking the silence.

"So," he says, crossing his arms, "I guess I'm your chauffeur now. From billionaire bad boy to driver."

There's a playful edge to his voice, but I can tell he's trying to lighten the mood, to push away whatever vulnerability slipped through during my little performance.

I raise an eyebrow, matching his tone. "Chauffeur, huh? You do have a nice car. I could always drive if you need a break."

He snorts.

"Nice car? This is a masterpiece on wheels, Arya...and nobody drives it but me."

Chapter Nine

ETHAN

AT ARYA'S INSISTENCE, we spend the night in separate hotel rooms, which irritates me but I let her have her way. She's feeling overwhelmed after everything that's happened between us and her encounter with those assholes in the bar parking lot. Lying in bed alone, I couldn't turn my mind off for a long time. I stared at the ceiling, thinking of Arya and the soft look she gave me as she teased me about chauffeuring her around. She'd wanted her own room though, and so now I'm not too sure where we stand.

Today, she's been quiet for most of the drive, gazing out the window at the passing scenery with a slightly furrowed brow, as if lost in thought. I want to know what's going through that pretty head of hers, but I've never been the type of man to grovel for a woman's attention, so I leave her to her musings.

We pull into the parking lot of the bar Arya's booked for her gig, and I can't help but wrinkle my nose at the sight. It's a dump—there's no other way to put it.

The neon sign flickers like it's on its last legs, and the building itself looks like it could use a good power wash and a fresh coat of paint. This is where she chose to play? I'm thrown off, to say the least. I can't wrap my head around why someone like Arya, with her talent and charm, would choose a place like this.

I glance over at her, but she appears unfazed. She's already gathering her things, ready to jump out and start setting up.

"Arya, you sure this is the right place?" I ask, my tone laced with skepticism. I thought the only reason she played in the first dive bar was because it was her hometown and her last hurrah before hitting the road to bigger and better things. Is she just going to keep playing in dumps like this the whole time?

She looks at me with a small smile, shrugging as if to say, *what did you expect?* "This is it. Don't let the outside fool you; the crowds here are always great."

I'm not convinced, but I bite my tongue. If she's comfortable here, I'll play along. Still, I'm not about to let her walk into this place alone. I get out of the car and walk around to her side, instinctively slipping into protective mode.

Inside, it's just as rough as the exterior suggested. The smell of stale beer hangs in the air, and the floors are sticky underfoot. The stage is small, barely more than a platform at one end of the room, and the sound equipment looks like it's been through hell and back. Arya doesn't seem to mind. She greets the sound techs with a grin, chatting with them as she starts setting up her violin.

I stand back, keeping an eye on things. I feel out of place in this dingy bar, but I'm not going anywhere. She's got a sound check to do, and I'll be damned if I'm going to leave her alone in a place like this. As she tunes her violin, I notice how she moves—effortless, confident, like this is where she belongs. Maybe she does, but that doesn't stop the unease from settling in my gut.

The last time I saw her on a stage, she was dressed in that ridiculous leotard. Right now, she's dressed in an oversized green sweater, holey jeans, and scuffed sneakers. She looks relaxed and comfortable, which is sexy in its own way.

When she's satisfied with the tuning, she reaches into her

bag and pulls out…a flip phone. I blink, not quite believing what I'm seeing. I mean, who even uses those anymore?

"What the hell is that?" I ask, trying to hide my surprise.

She glances up, casually flipping it open. "My phone? What about it?"

"It's ancient. Seriously, it's a dinosaur."

She laughs, like it's no big deal. "It works. What more do I need?"

I shake my head, trying to wrap my mind around it. I've got to admit, there's something almost endearing about it, but it also makes me realize how different our worlds are. It's a little uncomfortable because I take so much of my privilege and wealth for granted and I forget how good I've got it sometimes compared to other people.

The sound check wraps up and the techs call for a break. "Come on," I say, walking up to Arya and taking her arm gently but firmly. "We're going out."

She looks at me, confused. "Where?"

"You'll see."

I bundle her into the car, and she doesn't argue, though I can tell she's curious. The drive is short, just a few blocks down the road to the nearest phone store. I park, and she finally speaks up.

"Ethan, what are we doing here?"

"We're getting you a proper phone."

Her eyes widen. "Ethan, I can't afford a new phone. I don't need—"

"Yeah, you do," I cut her off, already getting out of the car. "And I'm paying for it, so come on."

She trails after me, half-protesting the whole way, but I'm not having any of it. This is non-negotiable. She can't keep going around with that relic in her pocket. She needs something more reliable. Something that won't drop calls, and can be tracked if, God forbid, an insane fan decides he wants to take her home with him.

Inside the store, I make quick work of picking out a phone.

"That one's way too expensive," she protests.

"I told you, I'm paying for it."

She lets out a huff of frustration. "You don't need to be dropping that kind of money on me!"

I ignore her as I go through with the purchase and get the phone set up with her number.

When I hand her the new phone, she looks down at it, then back at me, her expression softer now, maybe even a little grateful. "Ethan…you really didn't have to do this."

"I know," I reply, meeting her gaze steadily. "But I wanted to. You're going to need something reliable, especially on tour."

She gives me a considering look, as if trying to figure out what strings might be attached to this gesture.

"It's a gift," I assure her. "Don't overthink it. I don't want to have to hunt you down because your phone dies, so just be a good girl and take it."

She arches a brow at me and the corner of her mouth twitches, as though she's fighting a smile.

"I should chuck this phone at your head for that good girl comment alone," she laughs. Still, she accepts the phone without further argument. I can tell she's touched, even if she's trying to play it cool. And I feel something shift between us—a connection, maybe. It's subtle, but it's there.

As we head to the car, I feel oddly satisfied. I like that I was able to provide this for her. That, in a small way, I might be making her life a bit easier.

Once inside the car, I reach over and snatch the phone from her hand.

"What are you doing now?" she moans, annoyed.

"I'm going to be the first and most important number in your phone," I tell her, entering my contact information and setting it as a favorite in her contacts. Once I'm done, I give it back to her with a wink and she blushes as she takes it and ducks her head.

As soon as I start the car to head back to the bar, Arya is all business. She starts tapping away at the screen of her new phone, her fingers moving with surprising speed and precision for someone who just upgraded from a flip phone.

"What are you doing?" I ask as I pull away from the phone store and slip into traffic.

She doesn't look up at me as she answers, "setting up my social media apps. Filling in passwords, logging into accounts—it's going to be so nice not to have to rely on library computers or internet cafes to do all this."

"Library computers? Seriously?" I don't mean to sound as shocked as I do, but I can't help myself. I can't imagine not having access to my own laptop. It's a basic necessity.

She looks up at me, grinning. "You have no idea. This is going to save me so much time and hassle."

She's back at it, tapping away, and I can't help but be amused by how absorbed she is. I guess I underestimated how much she was struggling with that old flip phone. She's practically glowing now, and it's not just from the screen light.

Then she suddenly freezes, her finger hovering over the screen.

"Oh my, God," she says.

I tense, instantly on alert. "What is it?"

She looks at me, her eyes wide, but there's a spark of excitement there.

"I just got an email…the second violinist chair for Carnegie Hall is open for auditions! Oh, my God! Will you help me make an audition video and send it?"

"Second chair?" I echo, a bit confused. "Someone with your talent should be first chair."

She looks shocked and exclaims, "Ethan, it's Carnegie Hall! Even second chair is a huge deal. It's been a dream of mine forever, and honestly, it's a way to actually pay the bills and live in New York. It's a long shot to get any chair! I'm certainly not going to complain if I'm able to get second."

I suppose that makes sense. Still, she's got so much talent, she should be front and center in any performance she's part of.

It's not my world, and it's not my dream, so I don't voice my opinion any further and just nod. "Yeah, I can help you."

Back at the bar, Arya focuses on getting set up for her performance. She goes into the lady's room to change, and when she comes out, she's dressed in a neon green leotard with pink frills. Her makeup is just as bright, with green eyeshadow and pink cheeks. Her lips are a deep pink as well. Her look is wild, but perfect for her performance. Right before she's meant to go on, I notice her sliding a piece of newspaper out of her violin case and into the new phone case I bought her. I'm curious, but before I can ask, she gives me a quick smile and heads for the stage.

I make my way to a corner booth, settling in where I can keep a clear view of the stage and still be in position to step in if needed. The booth is surprisingly comfortable, considering the dive this place is. I pull out my phone and start checking my emails, figuring I might as well use the downtime productively and see if I've gotten a response about the trust yet.

Instead of the expected trust fund paperwork, however, I find an email from my father.

Ethan,

I must once again express my profound disappointment and concern regarding your marriage.

It is clear to me that this arrangement is nothing more than a facade, a decision driven by impulse rather than genuine commitment. You have made a mockery of the values we've always upheld, and I am getting tired of your constant need to rebel. Now you've married a low-class nobody who will embarrass our family and make a mockery of our public image.

In light of this, I must inform you that I am not prepared to transfer the funds from your trust at this time. "Choices have conse-

quences," as we have always said. This is not just about financial matters but about the kind of life you are choosing to lead, and it's my belief that you are too irresponsible to be given control of your trust. I will be working with my lawyer to overturn our agreement regarding your marriage and the trust. By the time you return home, this matter should be resolved.

Fuck! The nerve of him! He's really going to go this far because he doesn't approve of Arya? I've never been one to back down from a challenge, and if my father thinks he can control me through this, he's got another thing coming.

I feel a smirk form on my lips as I close the email. If Arya is causing this much of a stir, then maybe I should parade her around more. I like that idea, actually. Showing off my pretty, talented wife.

Pissing off my dad is just a bonus.

AS I STEP onto the stage, the lights hit me—pink, gold, and purple, casting a surreal glow over the crowd. I can't see much past the first few rows, but that's okay. The spotlight is my friend, wrapping me in its warmth, making the rest of the world disappear.

I close my eyes, just letting the music fill me, my fingers brushing over the strings of my violin like they've done a thousand times before. The crowd is rowdy and energetic, and I feed off of that. I'm playing one of my own pieces, something bright and bubbly on the surface, but with an undercurrent only I can feel.

As the first notes fill the room, I'm transported to another time, another place. The melody is light, almost playful, and the lyrics that dance in my mind are just as cheerful, but beneath it all, there's that ache, that gnawing sadness that never quite goes away. This song is about my brother and the pain I've experienced since we were separated. No one in this room would guess what this song really means to me. They hear the catchy tune, the upbeat rhythm, and they think it's all fun and games.

They don't know that my brother was wrongfully convicted and fucked over by the justice system, or that I was thrown into foster care as a result and got lost in the shuffle. I always believed I'd be able to find him after he got out of jail, and no matter how messed up he might have been, we'd be able to get through it as long as we were together again.

But then my backpack got stolen.

It was just a normal day, nothing special, until it wasn't. I was walking home from practice, my violin case slung over one shoulder, my backpack over the other. It happened so fast, I didn't even see the person's face. One moment it was there, the next it was gone—along with everything that mattered. The phone with the number he knew to call when he got out, the handwritten list of my dream performance venues...all of it vanished in an instant. Just like the person who stole it.

The crowd is with me now, caught up in the energy of the song. This place isn't anything like the venues I used to dream about. It's small, a little run-down, not exactly the bright lights and big city I imagined when I was younger, but it's a start, and with Ethan's help, maybe I'll actually make it to New York and Carnegie Hall.

As I perform, I can feel the crowd's eyes on me, but it feels like more than just the usual interest in the music. I feel that familiar thrill that makes me play faster and dance harder. My heart races and nothing else matters but the rush of performing.

When I finish the song, the applause is loud, enthusiastic even, but I can't shake the feeling that something else is going on. As I step off the stage, I hear snippets of conversation—my name, Ethan's last name, words like "marriage" and "court-house." It all clicks into place, and my heart sinks. Of course, they know. The news of our quickie courthouse marriage must have hit the local papers, and now everyone is here to see the woman who somehow landed herself in the Cavenwell family.

Great. Just great.

I do my best to keep smiling as I pack up my violin, trying to ignore the curious glances and whispered gossip. It's not like I can blame them; I'd probably be just as curious if I were in their shoes. Still, it makes me feel like a spectacle. They're here for the drama and not for the music. I can't let it get to me. This is just a small town stop, nothing more. I've got bigger dreams to chase, and I can't afford to get distracted by gossip. Besides, the bright side is I've probably gained fans and maybe a few social media followers.

With my violin safely packed away, I make my way to the bar to collect my payment. The owner, a grizzled old man with a permanent scowl, waits for me. I offer him my brightest smile, hoping to smooth over whatever mood he's in.

"Thanks for letting me play here tonight," I say, trying to keep my tone light and cheerful.

He grunts. "Yeah, about that…"

My stomach drops. "About what?"

The glint in his eyes makes my heart race. It's a look I've seen before. It's predatory and greedy. It's the look of a man who thinks he can take advantage of someone he perceives as weaker and more vulnerable.

"There's been a misunderstanding," he says, his voice dripping with false sympathy. "Seems like there's a clause in the contract you didn't notice. Your performance was supposed to bring in a minimum number of people and you fell short."

I blink, trying to process his words. "What are you talking about? There was no clause like that."

He shrugs, completely unfazed. "Guess you didn't read the fine print."

Panic rises in me, creeping up my throat and making it hard to breathe. I did read the contract, every word of it, but now he's telling me there's some hidden clause that means I don't get paid? This is my first stop on the tour…even if Ethan offered to pay for the tour, this is my first chance to make some money, and now it's slipping through my fingers.

I swallow hard, forcing myself to stay calm.

"I'm sure there's been a mistake," I say, my voice tight. I

gesture over my shoulder. "Besides, the bar is packed. Even if that clause existed, I clearly met the minimum crowd size."

The bar owner just smirks, leaning against the counter. "Sorry, those are the numbers."

The panic sharpens into something more like anger, but I keep it buried. I can't afford to lose my cool, not here, not now. What if this is how the whole tour goes? One disaster after another? I can't let that happen. I need this tour to work.

Just as I'm about to try another approach, a hand lands on my shoulder, firm and reassuring. I glance up to see Ethan standing beside me, his expression hard as he looks at the bar owner.

"Is there a problem here?" Ethan's voice is low, calm, but there's an edge to it that makes the bar owner's smirk falter.

The man's eyes dart nervously between Ethan and me as he realizes the weak little girl he assumed he could take advantage of isn't so defenseless after all. I can see the gears turning in his head, trying to figure out how to backtrack without looking like he's caving under pressure.

Ethan doesn't give him a chance.

"Behind the stage," Ethan growls. He lets go of my shoulder. "Stay here, Arya."

I watch, heart pounding, as the bar owner hesitates, then reluctantly shuffles toward the stage. Ethan follows, his posture relaxed but with an air of quiet authority that makes it clear he's not to be messed with. I wait until they disappear from sight before hurrying after them. Making my way behind the stage, I hide behind a speaker to try and listen to their conversation. I can see the tension in the way the bar owner's shoulders hunch, his mouth twisted into a sneer.

I catch the tail end of Ethan's words, his tone calm but carrying an unmistakable edge. "You'll pay her what she's owed, or I'll go to the police. I'm sure you don't want them sniffing around this place, do you?"

The bar owner scoffs, the sound ugly and dismissive. "You

think you can threaten me, pretty boy? You ain't scaring nobody."

Then, out of nowhere, the bar owner swings a punch at Ethan. My heart lurches in my chest, but Ethan moves like lightning, ducking the blow effortlessly. Before the bar owner can recover, Ethan grabs him by the arm and twists it behind his back, slamming him into the wall with a thud that echoes through the empty space.

"Let me go!" the bar owner snarls, his voice strained with pain and fear. He struggles against Ethan's hold, but it's no use. Ethan has him pinned, and there's a deadly calm in his eyes that makes the man's bravado crumble.

"You'll pay her," Ethan repeats. "Pay her what you owe her, or you'll be limping out of here while I bring every cop and trooper in a fifty mile radius down on your head. I doubt some of your regulars would like that, huh? How much money are you willing to lose just to be an asshole and not pay my wife what she's owed?"

I blink, caught off guard. He's handling this situation without dropping the Cavenwell name. That would be such an easy thing for him to do. Flex his wealth and hold it over the bar owner's head to force his hand. Instead, Ethan's relying on his own strength and handling this like any regular person might.

Saying that Ethan is a regular person is a stretch…he's intimidating as hell, with or without the Cavenwell name backing him up.

The bar owner nods frantically, the fight gone out of him in an instant as his face pales. "Okay, okay! I'll get the cash. Just let me go!"

Ethan holds him there for a moment longer, as if making sure the man understands, before releasing him. The bar owner stumbles away, rubbing his arm and muttering curses under his breath as he heads out toward the bar.

I step out from where I was hiding, my heart still racing from the sudden burst of violence. Ethan turns to look at me, and I'm struck by how calm and controlled he is. There's none of the arrogance and entitlement I would expect from someone who grew up in his world of privilege and power. It's surprising…but not an unwelcome one.

The bar owner returns with a stack of bills, his hands shaking as he counts out the money. He shoves it toward me without meeting my eyes, muttering something under his breath that I don't catch. I don't care. I take the money, stuffing it into my bag with a shaky breath of relief.

Ethan watches the whole exchange silently, his expression unreadable. When I finally look up at him, he's gazing down at me with a protective glint that makes me feel protected and safe. It's a strange feeling. Good, but strange. It's been a long time since anyone has truly made me feel secure and cared for. I have to remember not to get used to this. This arrangement is only temporary, and once it's over, Ethan will go off and live his life and I'll be alone again with only myself to rely on.

"Let's get out of here," he says quietly, slinging his arm over my shoulders possessively and pulling me close into his side as he turns to walk us out the bar door.

Chapter Eleven

ETHAN

THE COOL NIGHT air hits us as we step out into the alley. I take a deep breath, trying to steady myself, but it's not enough. I'm still struggling to get my temper under control so I don't go back into the bar and slam my fist into that asshole's face. It's only Arya's soft body pressed against mine that's keeping me from doing so.

"Does this happen often?" I ask.

She glances up at me. "What?"

"People trying to screw you over like that."

She shrugs and pulls her hair back, but she looks at her wrist and seeing no hair tie, releases her hair with an annoyed sigh. "I mean, not all the time, but now and then I'll have a jerk like that trying to take advantage of me just because I'm a young woman by myself. It sucks, but there's not always a lot I can do about it, you know?"

No, I don't know. I don't know what it's like to have someone rip me off because they think I'm too weak and vulnerable to do anything about it. My dad withholding my trust fund is not the same, and I'm not going to let him get away with it. I have resources and lawyers to fight the battle on my behalf.

Arya has no one, as far as I know, and next to nothing. Yet, she's still doing this. Still playing in these shithole venues because that's what she has to do in order to make her dream come true. Have I ever felt so passionately about something that I'd be willing to crawl through mud and shit to get it? Ever had a dream I was so determined to achieve, I'd put my wellbeing at risk? No...no, I haven't. Apart from getting my trust fund and getting out from under my dad's control, I really don't know what I want to do with my life. I want my freedom, to travel, and live however I choose to...but I have no specifics yet. It's all vague hopes and desires, but once I have my money, I don't have some tangible goal to work toward.

I've just been so consumed by my anger and frustration toward my family and their attempts to control me, I haven't really thought beyond them.

My mind flashes to the email from my father, the thinly veiled threats and condescension dripping from every line. Such a smug, arrogant bastard. He deserves to get knocked down a few pegs.

As we walk toward the car, Arya's got her phone out and is tapping away on the screen, her face screwed up in concentration.

"Hey, your phone all set up and working now?"

She looks up and gives me a grin that's almost bashful. "Yeah, mostly. Just have to finish a few things."

"Perfect," I say, an idea popping into my head. "Let's do something fun. How about featuring both of us on your social media? Make an official wedding announcement to your fans. You've got an audience now, and I think it's time they see who you married."

Arya looks at me, eyes narrowing slightly in confusion. "You really want to be in my posts?"

"Why not? I'm your husband, after all." The word feels strange in my mouth, but it also feels like the right move. If my father wants to question this marriage, I'll get so many people talking about it, he'll look foolish if he insists it's not real. A billionaire bachelor finally settling down will make tons of noise online and he won't be able to escape the sight of me and Arya together, no matter how much he tries.

Arya shrugs. "Alright. If you're sure about this?"

"Absolutely. If we're upfront about the marriage, it won't be such a big deal when we get to your venues. People will already have processed the news."

She looks thoughtful before nodding. "That makes sense. I would rather people focus on my music when they're at my shows and not speculate about my relationship status. Let's do it!"

We take a couple of pictures together, presenting ourselves as a happy couple. I put my arm around her shoulders in one picture, and kiss the top of her head in another. She flashes her ring, and I wrap my fingers around her wrist as if I'm holding up her hand. Once we've got a few, Arya messes with filters and captions and seems pleased with herself when she posts the pictures. As I watch her post the photos, I can't help but think how this will infuriate my father. A public reminder that I'm not following his script.

With that done, satisfaction flickers through me, but it's not enough to extinguish the frustration still boiling inside me. I lead Arya to the car, opening the door for her before sliding into the driver's seat. My hands grip the steering wheel a little tighter than necessary as I pull out of the parking lot.

The city streets blur past as I press harder on the gas, speeding through the night. The engine growls beneath us, and the rush of adrenaline feels good—like a release. It's not enough, though. I push the car faster, weaving through traffic.

"Ethan," Arya says quietly, breaking into my thoughts. "You might want to slow down."

I barely hear her. The frustration's too loud, buzzing in my ears like static. I take a sharp turn, the tires screeching against the asphalt. I just need to burn this off, to feel like I'm in control of something. The faster I go, the more the tension unwinds—until I hear her voice again, firmer this time.

"Ethan, slow down."

But I don't. Not yet. I can't. I need the speed. It's how I'll get this anger out of my system. Then I see the flash of red and blue in my rearview mirror. The police.

The lights swirl behind us, and the siren blares. My stomach sinks as reality crashes into place.

"Dammit," I mutter under my breath, finally easing off the gas. Arya's quiet beside me, but I can feel her eyes on me.

I pull over to the side of the road, the cop car stopping right behind us. The adrenaline that had been surging through me a moment ago turns cold. This is exactly what I don't need right now.

When the cop gets out of his car and starts walking to mine, I roll the window down.

"Evening, officer," I say with an exasperated sigh.

"Do you know how fast you were going, sir?"

I don't have time for this shit. "I'm guessing faster than I should?"

The cop gives me an annoyed frown. "Yeah, I'd say so. License, registration, and proof of insurance, please."

Digging out my wallet, I hand him my license and don't even bother pulling out my registration. The cop's eyes widen slightly when he sees my last name on the license. I've been through this routine more times than I can count—pulled over for speeding, the officer recognizes my last name, and suddenly everything's smoothed over.

"Just...just slow it down, Mr. Cavenwell," the officer says, handing me my license and tipping his hat before he strolls to his cruiser.

Gripping the wheel, I know I should feel relieved, but instead, there's this strange silence in the car, something thick in the air that I can't quite place. When I glance over at Arya, she's gone completely still, staring out the windshield, her jaw clenched.

"Arya?" I ask, but she doesn't respond right away. She doesn't even look at me.

Then, just like that, she turns toward me, her eyes blazing.

"What the hell was that, Ethan?"

Her voice is sharp, cutting right through the tension. I blink, taken aback for a second.

"What do you mean? It's fine, we're—"

"No, it's not fine!" She's glaring at me now, her voice shaking. "You can't just do whatever you want, Ethan. You were speeding, being reckless—like none of it matters, and you just assumed you could get away with it. Again." Her eyes narrow. "Because you always get away with it, don't you?"

I lean back, trying to figure out where this is coming from. "Look, I get it. I was driving too fast, but it's not a big deal. The cop barely cared—"

"Exactly!" she snaps. "That's the problem! You never think it's a big deal because you never face any consequences. You live in this bubble where your name gets you off the hook for everything. You don't understand how dangerous life can be for the rest of us."

"Dangerous? I'm not an idiot, Arya. I can handle a speeding ticket."

She throws her hands up. "It's not just about the ticket! It's about you thinking you can bend the rules whenever it suits you. You think you're untouchable, but you're just reckless. One wrong move and things could go sideways in a second, and it's not just your life, but my life you're putting in danger!"

Her voice cracks a little at the end, and for the first time, I realize she's not just angry—she's scared. Really scared.

I'm reeling, trying to process the shift from her usually calm demeanor. Where is this all coming from? It's a turn-on, to be honest, seeing her like this—so fierce, so damn sure of herself.

"Arya, I get it, okay? I messed up," I say, trying to cut through her tirade, but she's not having it.

"No, Ethan, you don't get it!" she shoots back, her voice rising. "How far are you willing to bend the rules? How far before you break something that can't be fixed?"

The air is electric between us, and suddenly I can't hold my temper back anymore.

"What about you, Arya?" I snap, turning to face her fully. "You want to talk about choices? Let's talk about this—your so-called dream tour. Think about the places you've booked. You're playing in total dives, with sleazy owners who don't even pay you until someone strong-arms them. This is what you want?"

"Yeah, well, at least I landed those gigs on my own merit and not because of my daddy's name!" she snaps. Clearly I've hit a nerve.

An uneasy silence falls between us as we glare at each other. Guilt starts gnawing at me, an unfamiliar feeling, and I know I went too far. Leaning back in my seat, I glance at her profile as she turns to stare out the window.

Shit.

"Look," I say at length, my voice tight. "I know you think I have it easy, and maybe I do. I've never had to stop bending the rules because things don't break for me. I've always been able to get what I want because of who I am, and I've probably taken that fact for granted, but you don't know shit about me or my life and what I've gone through to get to this point."

Her silence is almost worse than her anger. She doesn't turn to face me, just keeps her gaze fixed on the window. After a moment, she finally speaks, her voice steady but edged with bitterness.

"Things break for me all the time. I fight for everything I have. I scrape by and make do because I have no other choice. We can't all have a get out of jail free card. Bending the rules like that only works for rich people…and it's the rest of us that usually end up dealing with the consequences."

Her words hit me hard. This isn't just a complaint about society, this bitterness feels personal. There's something else going on here. Something I'm not seeing.

I want to argue, to defend myself, but the words get caught in my throat. She's right, in a way. I've never had to experience the grind, the constant struggle she faces. I've been shielded from the harsh realities of life that she deals with daily.

She's silent as I start driving again.

When we finally pull into the hotel parking lot, the tension between us is thick. We sit in silence, each lost in our thoughts. As I turn off the engine, I glance at Arya. She's already reaching for the door handle.

"I want separate rooms," she says firmly, without meeting my eyes as she climbs out of the car.

"Fine," I reply, feeling a mixture of relief and disappointment.

I get out of the car as well and we head inside, our steps echoing in the quiet lobby. She walks to the front desk, her shoulders tense, and my stomach twists with even more guilt. This entire situation is a mess—one I've largely caused with my reckless behavior and privileged attitude.

She receives her room key and heads off to the elevator, and I turn to the front desk to get my own room. The clerk hands me the key, and I make my way to the elevator, my mind still spinning from our conversation. I settle into my room, trying to shake off the frustration and guilt bearing down on me. Sitting on the edge of the bed, the door stares back at me as I wonder how I'm going to fix this thing I've so stupidly fucked-up.

What's really messing with me is that I care at all. I've never cared about anyone's opinion of me the way I seem to care about Arya's. Damn it! The whole point of this fake marriage was to disentangle myself from my family so I don't have to worry about what anyone thinks of me...to be free and on my own.

So why is it that I don't want to be free of her?

Chapter Twelve

ARYA

THE CAR ROLLS to a stop in front of the Walton's Coffee Shop in downtown Memphis. We've been driving all morning from Fort Smith, and I've done my best to ignore Ethan the entire way. I've been silent for the past few hours, refusing to talk to Ethan, my thoughts too tangled up to deal with him right now. Not after everything. Our fight from last night continues to play in my head, but as angry as I am with him, I'm almost angrier at myself. I was actually really starting to like Ethan, but last night, he acted like just another entitled, rich asshole.

I get out of the car, stunned. The coffee shop is a literal crime scene. The sun filters through the clouds, casting a gray light on everything, making the yellow police tape even starker. The windows of the shop are shattered, jagged shards of glass still hanging in the frames like broken teeth.

I was supposed to play here today, but that's clearly no longer happening. The sign on the door hangs crookedly, a hand-scrawled "Closed Due to Emergency" sign taped over it. People mill about, whispering to each other about what happened.

I'm still processing it. Ethan stands beside me, and I can feel his eyes on me.

"Well shit," I mutter. "What now?"

The glass crunches beneath my shoes as I step a little closer to the tape, peering through the broken window. Tables overturned, chairs knocked over. It doesn't take a detective to know someone had broken in, tearing the place apart. Shit. I bite my lip, frustration welling up inside me.

"Damn," Ethan mutters beside me. I ignore him, folding my arms tight around myself as the weight of disappointment presses down on me.

The shards of glass catch the sunlight, gleaming for a second like broken mirrors. I'm struck by the most intense feeling of deja vu as I take in the destruction. The broken glass. The yellow police tape. I've seen this before. I've *felt* this before.

My hand instinctively moves to the ring on my finger, the one I've barely thought about since Ethan slipped it on for our fake wedding. But now, the cool metal feels heavy, familiar in a way that makes my throat tighten. Images flash in my mind—photos I've tried to bury. Photos of broken windows, shattered glass, and the same damn yellow police tape. The day my brother was arrested.

I squeeze my eyes shut, willing the memories away, but it's too late. They're already flooding in.

The police had stormed into our house, accusing him of theft. They said they had evidence—broken windows, glass shards matching his fingerprints—that he robbed the Cavenwells. Lou's car had broken down and he'd been walking home through their neighborhood after dark when the robbery happened. Because he was a rough-looking stranger in a nicer area, he was immediately surrounded and assumed to be the thief. Lou tried to prove he didn't have anything to do with it, but Jared Cavenwell stepped in and insisted that Lou had done it. He had him thrown in jail, saying he was doing the world a favor by removing people like him off the street. My stomach tightens and I think I might be sick but I manage to keep the contents of my stomach down.

My pulse quickens when I slip my hands into my bag, digging deep as I brush the edge of my phone. Pulling it out, I flip it over and pop the case open, revealing the folded piece of paper I've hidden in there. My throat tightens as I smooth it out with trembling hands, my heart pounding in my chest.

It's just a small clipping—old, yellowed around the edges—but the words printed on it have haunted me since the day my brother was arrested. I keep it as a reminder of the nightmare we lived through, a reminder that people like them destroy lives without a second thought.

"Robbery Shakes Prominent Dallas Family: Cavenwells Targeted in High-Value Heist"

Dallas, TX — In a shocking turn of events, the Cavenwell family, well-known philanthropists and owners of one of Dallas' most prestigious real estate firms, were the victims of a robbery at their Highland Park estate late Friday night. Authorities confirmed that a significant amount of cash, jewelry, and other valuables were stolen during the heist, with estimated losses reaching over $500,000.

According to police reports, the burglar gained entry through a back window, bypassing the security system. The Cavenwells were reportedly not at home at the time of the robbery. The stolen items include a number of rare, custom pieces of jewelry, some of which are said to be family heirlooms with high sentimental value.

The Dallas Police Department launched an immediate investigation and arrested a suspect found wandering through the neighborhood. The young man, Louis Winston, was taken into custody after he was identified by Senator Jared Cavenwell.

My eyes skim over the familiar lines about the theft and the so-called evidence. But what makes my stomach twist is the photo at the bottom. A grainy black-and-white image of the stolen jewelry. The same jewelry they used to frame my brother. Displayed prominently among the pieces is an antique ring...

My eyes fall to the ring on my finger, the one Ethan slipped on so casually when we got married. My heart stops. I can't breathe.

It's the ring from the picture. The ring that was supposedly stolen that night—the Cavenwells had it this whole time! The delicate band, the intricate details…it's all clicking into place now. I swallow hard, my pulse racing as I stare at it, the weight of it suddenly unbearable.

Jared Cavenwell *knew* Lou was innocent—he set my brother up.

"Hey, you okay?" Ethan asks. I glance up at him but his furrowed brow of concern irritates me and I quickly look away.

"I'm fine," I murmur. Shoving the clipping back into the case, my hands shaking. I can't escape the truth now. I'm wearing the very thing that was used to tear my family apart. The same ring that put my step-brother behind bars for something he didn't do.

My breath comes in shallow bursts as I try to make sense of everything. I can't believe I let myself be vulnerable with Ethan. I can't believe I let my guard down, even for a second. I thought maybe, just maybe, there was more to him than his name. That he wasn't just another cold, calculated Cavenwell. There were moments—small, fleeting moments—when I felt something shift between us, when I thought maybe he was different from the rest of them.

I can't even look at the ring without my stomach turning. It's like a noose around my finger, tightening with every passing second, reminding me of everything I've lost, of everything my brother lost because of *them*. I clench my fists, digging my nails into my palms as the anger boils up inside me. I grab the ring and yank it off my finger. I'm tempted to throw it as far as I can, but I stop myself and instead stuff it into my pocket.

I'm not just angry—I'm furious. At myself, at Ethan, at the entire situation. I trusted him, even if I didn't want to admit it. I let myself believe that maybe he wasn't like the rest of his family. That he could be different, but I should've known better.

I should've known that people like him—people with power, with money, with influence—they take what they want, and they leave destruction in their wake. Just like his family did to mine.

I've been walking around with my brother's past wrapped around my finger, thinking I was in control. Thinking I could handle this. But I was wrong. So damn wrong.

I've let Ethan in once, but never again. Not after knowing what I know now. Not after remembering what this ring—and everything it stands for—has cost me.

"I'm going to talk to the cop over there," Ethan says, nodding toward a police officer standing on the sidewalk, appearing to guard the taped off coffee house. "See what all happened."

"Sure, you do that."

When he reaches the cop and is distracted, I turn and march away. The hotel we're staying at is within walking distance, so I grab my bag and violin cases out of Ethan's car and head that way.

I just need space. Space to think, to breathe. Away from him.

The hotel looks quieter than I expected, almost peaceful compared to the mess of emotions swirling inside me. I head inside, already mentally planning to lock myself in my room and figure out how I'm going to confront Ethan about this. There's no way in hell I'm staying in the marriage if he actually knows about what happened to Lou; if he is in on it with the rest of his family. Who knows, maybe it's some big joke that they laugh at when they're gathered for holidays and Sunday dinners.

I walk up to the front desk, forcing myself to sound calm, even though my nerves are still humming. "Arya Jones. Checking in."

The clerk glances at the screen, his fingers tapping against the keyboard. Then he gives me a polite smile.

"Ah, yes. We have you under a shared reservation—one room."

I blink, my mind stumbling over his words. "What? No, that's not right. I booked a separate room."

He gives me that customer-service smile again, like he deals with confused people all the time. "It looks like your reservation for a separate room was canceled earlier. It's now under one room, with Mr. Ethan Cavenwell."

Of course. Of *course* he canceled my room.

A wave of anger surges through me, so sharp it nearly knocks the air from my lungs. My hands curl into fists at my sides. Ethan. I can't believe I agreed to this ridiculous plan. I can't believe I thought for even a second that I could trust him.

"Thanks," I grit through clenched teeth, grabbing the room key from the clerk before storming off toward the elevator.

The elevator doors slide open, and I step inside, staring blankly at my reflection in the mirrored walls. The girl staring back looks calm, composed, when in reality, I'm unraveling.

As soon as I make it to the room I drop my bag onto the bed without a second glance. The space feels suffocating, even though it's large and well-kept. But it's not *my* space. It's his. I haphazardly pull clothes from my suitcase until I find something I can work out in and change. I grab my headphones and a water bottle and head straight for the hotel gym. I need to burn off this rage. Sprint on a treadmill until I'm so exhausted, I don't have the strength to kill Ethan when I see him again.

Though I doubt that I won't still try.

Chapter Thirteen

ETHAN

I TURN to say something to Arya and realize she'd left the coffee shop while I was talking to the cops. Panic rushes me, but I tamp it down, reminding myself this is exactly why I'd gotten her that new phone. Pulling up the finder app on my own device, it pings her location at the hotel. A relief, yes, but definitely something we're going to have to talk about because I can't have her running off like this again.

When I make my way up to our room, I'm not really surprised that Arya isn't there. I didn't figure she'd be sitting around waiting for me to get back, but not knowing where she is has me concerned. Something happened at the coffee shop. I don't know what, but the look on her face...

I need to find her. Now. She has to be in the hotel somewhere. The clerk at the front desk confirmed that she checked in, and I can't imagine she'd just take off again on her own after doing so.

Even as I tell myself this, a voice in the back of my head whispers that she could've just left. She doesn't need me...not really. She's smart, tough, and is used to looking out for herself. If she wanted, she could easily make it on her own. Remembering what she said about using library computers, I make my way to the hotel's business center to see if she's there, even though she has her new smartphone. The pool is my next stop, but she's not there either. Since the hotel's gym is nearby it won't hurt to check there too.

She's lost in her own world, earbuds in, moving fluidly through a series of yoga poses in front of a large mirror across the room, near a couple of treadmills. I stop in the doorway, just watching her, mesmerized. She's dressed in tight, black yoga pants and a bright yellow sweatshirt, and her hair is pulled back, a few loose strands sticking to her face. She looks alive and focused, with her flushed cheeks and narrowed eyes as she studies her form in the mirror.

Watching her now, it's like she's forgotten all the tension between us, forgotten how pissed off she was when she stormed off earlier. Hell, maybe she *has* forgotten for a while. She seems so at ease now, her body movements graceful and fluid.

She's so fucking sexy, my cock twitches, imagining the things I want to do to her luscious little body. I want to bend her forward so she's pressed against the mirror while I take her from behind. She'd probably slap me if I tried.

Movement out of the corner of my eye catches my attention, and I spot some gym bro watching her too closely from his spot by the weights. His eyes linger on her in a way that sets my teeth on edge, and a flicker of possessiveness surges through me.

I send him a sharp glare, locking eyes with him until he looks away, quickly finding something else to focus on. Good call, buddy.

Turning away from the guy, I head toward the arm machine, shrugging off my jacket and draping it over the back of a nearby bench. She's still moving, still lost in the music, and I settle into the machine, starting a set while keeping my eyes on her. I know I should be focused on the reps, but it's hard to look away.

She's not just attractive—she's stunning. There's something raw and real about her that I never see in the women I date. I sit back on the bench, my eyes still glued to Arya as she moves through another slow, deliberate pose. I've seen her light up the stage with that bright, infectious energy she always carries. She's got this way of making everyone around her believe she's all sunshine—easygoing, carefree, like nothing in the world could touch her, but watching her now, really watching her, I see something else.

There's more to her than I realized. Much more.

My pulse quickens as she finishes, finally noticing me watching her. Her eyes meet mine, and I can see the shift—her walls come back instantly. She doesn't say anything, just packs up her things, but this moment isn't going to slip by. If I don't try to at least try to get her to open up, it's going to be impossible to fix anything between us.

I stand up, wiping the sweat from my forehead with the back of my hand, and make my way over to her. My muscles are still tight from the workout, and I probably look like a mess, but I don't care. She pulls her earbuds out and looks me up and down. Checking me out?

"Let's head upstairs," I say, my voice softer than usual, trying not to spook her.

Her expression is guarded but not hostile. That's a start. Without a word, she nods. The walk to the elevator is quiet, too quiet, and by the time the doors slide open and we step inside, the silence feels suffocating. I press the button for our floor, and we stand there, side by side, the awkward tension filling the space between us.

I steal a glance at her, hoping she'll say something—*anything* —to break the dead air, but she just stares straight ahead, her arms folded across her chest. I've never seen her like this—so closed off, so distant. It's driving me crazy.

Taking a deep breath, I try to calm my racing thoughts. I could apologize now, try to smooth things over, but I don't even know where to start. I've been frustrated with her, frustrated with the way she's been insisting on separate rooms, with the way she's shut me out without telling me why. Canceling her room was, admittedly, a little childish of me, but if it gets out that we're not in the same room together, our whole plan will go up in smoke. The perception that our marriage is real and solid is important.

And, if I'm being honest, I want her to talk to me. If she keeps hiding away from me, we're not going to work through this and the rest of this tour is going to be awkward and tense as fuck.

The elevator dings, and we step out, the silence following us down the hall like a shadow. I walk beside her, my mind buzzing as we get closer to the room. We reach the door, and Arya pulls out the keycard, sliding it into the lock.

She opens the door, and as soon as we're inside, the door clicks shut behind us. The air between us feels thick and charged with everything unsaid between us.

I can't take it anymore. If I don't say something now, I know I'll regret it.

I run a hand through my hair, still damp from the workout, and let out a breath I didn't realize I was holding.

"Arya," I start, my voice softer than usual, "we need to talk."

She doesn't say anything, just stands next to the bed, her back to me. I step closer, the tension in my chest tightening as I search for the right words.

"I wanted to say that I understand that I take my privilege for granted, That the world I grew up in and the one you grew up in are very different, but you're helping me see things differently. I need you to know that."

Arya still faces the bed, her hands gripping the edge, but I can see the way her posture eases, the way her fingers loosen. She's listening, even if she's not ready to respond yet.

I take another step toward her, closing some of the distance between us. My throat breaks as I speak, but I push forward.

"You're capable of great things, Arya, and I'm sorry if I've ever made you think I don't believe that."

Her head dips slightly, and she takes a breath, but doesn't look my way. Another step closer, enough now that I could reach out and touch her, but I don't. Not yet.

"When I see you up there on stage, when I watch you play, I see someone who can take on the world. Someone who doesn't need anyone telling her how great she can be because she already knows it."

Arya's breathing is steady, but I can see the way she's holding herself—guarded, like she's still not sure whether to let me in or push me away again. And honestly, I wouldn't blame her for either.

Finally, after what feels like an eternity, she turns around to face me. "I don't even care about any of that anymore," she says, her tone sharp.

I frown, confused. "What? I thought…last night…and when you left the coffee shop…"

She pulls her phone case out of her back pocket and digs something out of the case. I realize it's the paper I saw her move from her violin case at her show last night. She crosses to me and shoves the paper in my hand. When I look down at it, I'm stunned. It's a newspaper article about the robbery that took place at my family's house in Dallas six years ago. Furrowing my brow, I look up at Arya.

"Why do you have this?" I ask.

She doesn't answer and instead moves to her violin case and pulls my grandmother's ring out of it. Holding it up, she hisses, "Why did you give me this ring?"

"It was my grandmother's. A family heirloom. I thought…"

"You thought what?" She's clearly angry, and I'm clearly missing something. "You thought you could throw this in my face? Taunt me with this?" She shakes the ring. "With the con that put my brother in prison?"

I shake my head and hold up my hands. "Hold on! I have no idea what's going on right now. Your brother's in prison? Who the hell is your brother?"

"Louis Winston," she growls.

I look down at paper, then up to her again.

"Wait…your brother is the guy who robbed my family?"

"No!" she exclaims. "He didn't do it. He was set up! Your family framed him and sent him to prison, and you have the nerve to give me this goddamn ring? I thought you were different from the rest of them, but this is just cruel—"

"Slow down," I insist in as calm of a tone as I can manage. "You're not making sense. I had no idea you were Winston's sister. You don't have the same last name."

"He's not my biological brother," she snarls. "But he was more family to me than my own mother was."

"Okay, I get that. Now, as for the ring, I wasn't even around when the robbery happened. I was getting kicked out of college in a totally different state. Whatever happened that day, I had absolutely nothing to do with."

"Look at the picture in the paper. That's the jewelry your father claimed my brother stole."

I look at the image on the page in my hand, and sure enough, my grandmother's ring is among the items pictured.

"Look, the only reason I gave you that ring was because I thought it would piss my dad off," I tell her. "I snagged it before any of my brothers and took it out of my parents' safe. I swear to God, Arya, I couldn't have known this ring was involved in the robbery."

She stares up at me for several moments and, to my shock, tears start pooling in her eyes. I'm completely out of my depth. My family has caused enough damage, and now this? Framing an innocent person for theft? Because they sure as hell had the jewelry this whole time. I saw several of those pieces in the safe when I grabbed the ring.

I can't believe my father did this. It's one thing to fuck with my life, but Arya's? This shit with my dad isn't just business, it's personal. For me and for her.

I reach out and grab her hand, squeezing it, and she looks up at me, her face twisted with frustration and grief.

"Lou didn't do it," she whispers. "He didn't. I know he didn't."

My mind races, trying to piece together how the hell we ended up here. I'm shocked, confused, but more than anything, I feel this overwhelming urge to fix it. To do something. Not just because of the ring or the robbery, but because it's Arya. The idea of her carrying this weight alone—it's unbearable.

"Look," I say, my voice steadying as I make a decision. "I don't know what the hell happened with that robbery, but I swear I'll help you figure it out. We'll get to the bottom of this."

Arya blinks, clearly surprised by my words, but I'm already making up my mind. This is just one more reason to stay far away from my family, especially my father. They've already messed up enough lives, and if I can do something to stick it to them—while helping Arya—I'm all in.

She's still looking at me, tears in her eyes, and I can't help but feel this surge of protectiveness. This is more than just our arrangement now. I don't care if it's complicated, or if it means digging into old family wounds, I'm going to help her.

"Ethan," she whispers, her voice shaky. "Are you sure?"

Her hand is warm in mine when I squeeze it. "Yeah, Arya. I'm sure. I'm going to help you find out the truth. And I'm going to help clear your brother's name."

"No one ever believed me and Lou. No one offered to help." To my surprise, she cups the side of my face and pushes onto her toes to press her lips against mine, letting out a small sob of relief. The kiss is soft and sweet, but it sparks something inside me. Something hot and hungry. She pulls back, but I'm not nearly satisfied. I wrap my arm around her waist and pull her tight against me. Her eyes go wide and she lets out a gasp.

"What are you doing?" she breathes.

"Something I've been wanting to do for a long time," I say before pulling her in and kissing her again.

This kiss is not soft and sweet. It's demanding and rough, but I can't help myself. She tastes so sweet and I want her to submit to me. To give herself over completely so we can both finally do what we've been dancing around since we started this whole thing. She tenses and I wonder if she's going to push me away, but she melts into me. She slides her arms up around my neck and holds onto me as she parts her lips to let my tongue slip into her mouth. Groaning, I drop my hands to her hips and start backing her up toward the bed.

When we reach the bed, I grab the bottom of her bright yellow sweatshirt and yank it up and over her head. She gasps when I slip my hands below the waistband of her yoga pants to cup her perky little ass. Arya starts tugging at my shirt, practically clawing at it, as if she could shred it to pieces to get it off me.

Once my shirt is gone, she runs her hands up my chest, seeming to savor the feel of my muscles. Her cheeks are flushed and her eyes glassy with lust.

"Get on the bed."

Biting her lip, she obeys, sitting on the edge of the mattress. Dropping to my knees in front of her, I grip her yoga pants and pull them down her legs. She lets out a quick breath, and once she's in nothing but her sports bra and underwear, I take hold of her ankle and run my fingers up the inside of her calf, making her shiver.

"Ethan," she murmurs.

"Just relax, I've got you," I tell her, lifting her leg and kissing the inside of her thigh.

She whimpers and lets her legs fall open even more.

I like this. I like that she's not playing coy and that she's totally open and honest about her desires.

"You're so beautiful." I kiss further up her thigh. "Do you know how crazy you make me?"

She shakes her head. "As crazy as you make me?"

I chuckle with my lips pressed against her skin. "I'm glad it's not just me."

She combs her fingers through my hair and I look up at her.

"I've never had someone affect me this way," she admits in a soft voice. "It…it's kind of frightening."

Straightening, I wrap my arms around her waist and turn my face up to hers.

"I understand." I press a kiss against her chest, between her breasts. "I've never felt this way about someone before either. I'm not sure what it means, exactly, but I don't want to resist it."

"Me either," she replies, sliding her hands down either side of my face and then to my shoulders.

"Good." Hooking my fingers around her panties, I slide them down her legs. Pressing her knees apart, I lower my head to her pretty pussy and drag my tongue along her folds.

Arya throws her head back and lets out a long moan.

"I love how you taste," I growl.

She hooks her legs around my shoulders and pulls me closer. I lick and kiss her pussy, savoring the sound of her whimpers and groans. She falls against the bed and starts undulating her hips against me. I tighten my hold on her and hold her so she can't move as I wrap my lips around her clit and start sucking.

Arya lets out a cry and thrashes her head back and forth.

"Oh, my God! Ethan!"

I suck harder, loving the sounds she makes when she's close to coming. She continues to writhe and squirm and I slip a finger inside her. She lets out a whimper, her channel squeezing around me so perfectly my cock throbs.

I'm barely holding onto my self-control, but I want her to

come before I fuck her. Reaching up with one hand, I shove her sports bra up, revealing her perfect, perky breasts.

She's gorgeous, her face flushed, her nipples pink and hard, her lips parted in pleasure.

"Ethan…Ethan…oh, I'm close!" she gasps and I add a second finger as I continue licking and sucking at her sensitive little clit.

Within moments, her body seizes and she's screaming my name, her thighs squeezing my head as she grinds against my face.

I can't hold back anymore. Taking my fingers out of her, I move up, covering her body with mine and stealing her lips in a heated kiss. As our tongues tangle, I undo my jeans and shove them down my legs, along with my boxer briefs. Continuing to kiss her, I take hold of my cock and stroke it before lining it up with her entrance.

I gaze down into her eyes.

"Keep your eyes on me," I order.

She nods and wraps her arms around my neck as I push my hips forward and slide into her.

Arya lets out a needy cry and I brace my hands on either side of her head and begin moving my hips.

"Fuck, Arya," I growl. "You feel so good. So tight and perfect."

"You're so deep," she practically pants. Her fingers dig into me, holding me tight so I can't get away from her.

I move faster and harder until I'm pounding into her mercilessly. She cries out in pleasure, wrapping her legs around me, her head thrashing back and forth. It's wild and raw and the hottest thing I've ever experienced.

Reaching between us, I press my thumb to her clit and rub it in hard circles.

"Fuck!" she shouts. "Ethan! I'm…I'm coming!"

Her whole body seizes and she's suddenly squeezing me so tight, I can't hold back any longer. Throwing back my head, I let out a roar as I come deep inside her. Stars explode in my vision and it feels like I'm being torn apart and put back together from the inside out. It's the most intense pleasure I've ever experienced and I'm happy to lose myself to it completely. Nothing else matters to me in this moment but me, Arya, and our shared ecstasy.

I don't know how much time passes before the waves of pleasure start to slow and I come back down to earth. I collapse to the bed next to her, gently pulling out of her as I do so. We lay there in silence for long moments, our breathing heavy as the aftershocks move through us.

"Holy shit," I murmur at length.

"Yeah," she gasps. "That was…intense."

I turn my head toward her and pat my chest. "Come here."

She gives me a surprised look but moves closer, snuggling into my side and laying her head over my heart. I wrap my arm around her and hold her, not ready to be separated from her luscious body.

It's almost shocking how perfectly she fits against me. Like she was made just for me. I squeeze her closer, struck with a strange sense of…belonging. As if I'm meant to be here with her. It's confusing, but I don't dislike the feeling. It's grounding in a way. I feel like I have a purpose for the first time in a long time, and it's to be at Arya's side.

"Ethan…" she whispers, but I gently shush her, overwhelmed by my sudden feelings.

"Don't think about it," I tell her. "Don't think about anything. Just rest. You've still got a performance tonight. You need to be at your best."

She's tense for several seconds before she relaxes in my arms and I know, for the moment, nothing else matters but the two of us.

Chapter Fourteen

THE NIGHT AIR in Memphis is thick with cigarette smoke and the low hum of voices. The bar is dimly lit, hazy, with the soft clinking of glasses and distant laughter drifting through the air. It's not glamorous, not by a long shot, but the energy is real, raw, and I like that. I glance around the venue, taking in the peeling posters on the walls, the worn-out bar stools, and the stage tucked away in the corner.

Ethan is by my side. The atmosphere between us has shifted. I still can hardly believe we had sex earlier, but it feels like some of the tension that's been lingering between us since we met has eased and I'm able to relax a bit in his presence. Just a bit because whenever I think about what he did to me in our hotel room, my whole body goes tense with need and desire.

More than the intense sex is this sense that I'm not…alone. Ethan didn't know about the jewels and his dad setting Lou up to take the fall for the theft. He believes me. No one has believed me in the six years since Lou was locked up. I've been so alone for so long that having someone in my corner feels strange, but good. Very, very good.

His phone buzzes, the screen lighting up, and I catch the

brief flicker of annoyance in his eyes before he steps away to answer it.

"I'll be right back," he says, already moving toward the back of the room where the noise is thinner. I watch as he holds the phone to his ear, his jaw tight as he speaks.

I know exactly who's calling. His father. I can practically feel the tension radiating off him from across the room, the weight of whatever is being said on the other end of the line pulling him in deeper. It's always the same—his father dangling that damn trust fund over his head, trying to control him with the promise of money and power. I can't hear the conversation, but I don't need to. I know what it sounds like by now.

Choices have consequences, son. That phrase alone grates on my nerves.

While Ethan paces at the edge of the room, his voice low and tense, I head toward the stage. I've still got time before I go on, but I want to get a feel for the place, and maybe shake off the strange mix of emotions still swirling inside me. We crossed a line—one we'd been dancing around for a while. Now that we've slept together, things feel…different. Like I've let him in more than I intended. Like I'm in deeper than I thought I'd ever be. I'm starting to rely on him, which isn't something I've done since Lou was put away. I've been on my own for so long, it's strange to have someone by my side who I can turn to. Who I can trust.

But can I trust him, really? Am I being naive, believing Ethan so readily?

I push those thoughts aside for now. I can't afford to get too wrapped up in it, not with the set I have to focus on tonight.

Up near the stage, a woman adjusts her mic stand, her warm-up notes cutting through the air with effortless precision. She's striking, with her dark hair pulled into a tight ponytail, and she moves with a confidence that catches my attention. I don't recognize her at first, but she's clearly a seasoned pro. She looks to be in her early thirties, probably, so maybe about ten years older than me.

I can only imagine how much experience she's gotten in this industry.

"You must be Arya," she says, noticing me standing nearby. "I've heard good things. I'm Portia, by the way, but you can call me Tish." She flashes me a friendly smile, and I instantly feel at ease.

I smile back, walking closer. "Yeah, that's me. You sound great. Are you performing tonight too?"

She nods, adjusting her mic. "Yeah, just a short set before you go on. I mostly perform in Nashville, but I'm here to test out some new stuff before heading back."

Nashville. The word hits me like a jolt of electricity. My final stop on this tour. The place where everything either falls into place or crumbles apart.

"I'm heading to Nashville for my last gig," I tell her, unable to keep the hint of nervousness out of my voice.

Tish raises an eyebrow, her expression curious. "First time playing there?"

I nod, feeling sheepish. "Yeah, it's kind of a big deal for me. Any advice?"

She grins, leaning in like she's about to share some secret wisdom. "Don't let the place get in your head. Everyone there's chasing the same dream, but the key is to keep doing *your* thing. Don't worry about what everyone else is doing or what the audience expects. Stay true to your sound, your story. That's what'll set you apart."

Her words sink in, and I feel a small sense of relief. Maybe I've been overthinking Nashville, putting too much pressure on myself to make everything perfect. But hearing it from someone who's been there, who's done it, makes me think maybe I just need to trust myself a little more.

"Thanks," I say, meaning it. "I needed to hear that."

Tish smiles again, more softly this time. "No problem. It's

tough out there, but if you've got the passion, people will see it. The struggle doesn't stop after the tour, though. There's always another mountain to climb."

The weight of her words settles over me. The struggle doesn't stop. I know that. If I can't make this work, then what? How long will it last before I'm back to scraping by again, trying to fulfill my dream? I haven't let myself dwell on it much, but now, standing here in this smoke-filled bar, it feels impossible to ignore.

Tish looks like she's got it together—experienced, successful, confident in what she's doing—but she's still here, hustling. Still fighting to stay afloat in an industry that doesn't care how much you've already put in, and I'm just starting to realize how much further I have to go.

I glance over my shoulder toward Ethan, who's still deep in conversation, his expression hard as he talks to his father. We both have our battles to fight, our own struggles pulling us in different directions, but for the first time, I start to wonder if my dream—my music—is something I can truly make a living off of.

Tish clears her throat, snapping me out of my thoughts.

"You'll be fine," she says with a knowing smile. "Nashville's a beast, but if you've made it this far, you've got what it takes."

I nod, grateful for the encouragement. "Thanks, Tish. I appreciate it."

She gives me a wink before turning to her mic, and I step back, taking a deep breath as I mentally prepare myself for the set ahead. There's so much swirling in my mind, but tonight? Tonight is about the music. Everything else can wait.

As I look toward Ethan, still caught in that tug-of-war with his father, I know that I'll have to figure out my next steps soon, but for now, I have a show to play.

————

Electric energy fills the bar, buzzing with the aftermath of the performance. I'm still riding high from the set, adrenaline pumping through my veins as I lean against the bar, smiling wide. The crowd was all in tonight—cheering, clapping, even singing along at points. I nailed it. Every note, every beat. It feels like everything I've worked for is finally starting to pay off.

Tish sidles up next to me, her phone in hand. I invited her up to sing a couple numbers with me, and having her performing alongside me was incredible. We fed off each other's energy and I poured everything I had into the show.

"You crushed it out there, girl," she says, grinning as she pulls up one of the videos we shot earlier. "We gotta share this —tag each other, get that social media hype going."

I nod eagerly, already pulling out my phone. We swap handles, and within minutes, we're sharing clips of the performance, the comments and likes starting to pour in almost immediately. It feels good—better than good. Like the momentum I've been building for so long is finally taking shape, and I'm not just another girl with a dream. I'm *doing* it.

As we finish posting, I glance around the bar. It's packed, people are still buzzing from the show, and Ethan is standing just behind us, keeping an eye on the crowd like some kind of silent bodyguard. His gaze sweeps the room, but when it lands on me, he relaxes slightly, giving me a small nod as if to say, *I've got this covered.* He's been watching out for us all night, making sure we've got space at the bar, keeping anyone from getting too close. It's sweet, in a quietly protective way.

It's hot as hell in the packed bar and I lift my hair off my neck to try to cool down. Ugh. *Why do I never have a ponytail holder when I need it?*

Ethan leans and speaks in my ear. "Do you need to put your hair up?"

Surprised, I arch a brow. "I wish, but I lost my damn elastic...again."

He removes a black hair band from around his wrist and hands it to me. I stare at it before taking it.

He's been holding onto this for me? My heart flutters and I turn my gaze up to him.

"Thanks."

"You're welcome," he says.

Using the hair tie, I quickly pull my hair back and sigh in relief as air reaches the back of my sweaty neck. Grateful for his thoughtfulness, I lean against him slightly, feeling a bit light-headed from the performance and the couple of drinks I've already had.

"What are you drinking?" I ask, peering at the bottle in his hand.

He lifts the beer, taking a swig.

"Just a beer," he says casually, but I narrow my eyes at him.

"*Just a beer*?" I tease, grinning up at him. "Come on, Ethan. I know you better than that. This is way too tame for you."

He raises an eyebrow, and I can see the faint hint of a smirk tugging at his lips. "You think so, huh?"

Before I can respond, Tish pipes up from the other side of me, her eyes glinting mischievously.

"Oh, we're not letting you get off that easy," she says, turning toward the bartender. "Three picklebacks!"

The bartender chuckles and shakes his head but starts prepping the drinks. I laugh, shaking my head.

"Oh, you're getting us into trouble, Tish."

"Trouble's where the fun is," she replies with a wink, handing one of the shots to me, another to Ethan, and keeping one for herself.

We lift the shots, clinking them together in a sloppy toast before downing the whiskey and chasing it with the pickle juice. The salty burn hits hard, and I can't help but scrunch my face up, laughing through the sting as Tish whoops beside me.

Ethan winces but downs his shot like a pro, shaking his head with a grin.

"You happy now?" he asks, looking down at me.

"Very," I reply, the alcohol making me bolder than usual. "You're way too serious. Loosen up."

But before Ethan can respond, the bartender leans across the counter, sliding a drink over to Tish and flashing a charming grin at both of us.

"Next round's on me, ladies," he says smoothly, his gaze lingering on me a little too long.

Ethan's mood shifts instantly. I can feel the change in the air before I even turn to look at him. His jaw clenches, his hand tightening subtly around his empty beer bottle.

"Appreciate the offer," he says, his voice low, "but my *wife* is good."

The bartender's smile falters as his eyes flick to Ethan, clearly sizing him up. He takes a step back, nodding quickly.

"Didn't mean anything by it, man."

Ethan doesn't respond, but he's still staring the guy down until he moves away to another part of the bar. The tension in his posture eases, but that protective edge lingers around him.

Tish's eyes slide over to me, catching the shift in my expression. She notices the way I fiddle with the ring on my finger—the ring Ethan put on me, the ring I've barely been able to stop thinking about since Memphis. I twist it around absentmindedly, my mind going back to everything I've been trying to push away. The deal, the fake marriage, the ring that feels like a weight I wasn't expecting to carry.

"I'm going to the bathroom," Ethan whispers in my ear. "Don't move from this spot, and if anyone offers you a drink, don't take it. I'll be right back."

Ethan steps away to go to the restroom, and I take a deep breath and lean against the bar, swirling my drink and trying to distract myself from the thoughts swirling in my head.

Tish bumps my shoulder with hers and raises an eyebrow.

"So, what's really going on, Arya?" she asks, her tone playful but laced with concern.

I blink, caught off guard. "What do you mean?"

She gives me a knowing look, eyes flicking to my hand where I'm still fiddling with my ring. "You keep playing with that ring like it's burning a hole in your finger. Spill."

I bite my lip, looking down at the ring again, twisting it around absently. I want to brush her off, tell her it's nothing, but Tish doesn't seem like the type to let things slide. And, honestly? I'm tired of carrying this secret around. It's starting to feel like a weight I can't ignore anymore.

With a sigh, I lower my voice and glance toward the restroom, making sure Ethan isn't back yet.

"Okay," I say. "The marriage…it's fake."

Tish's eyes widen, her face scrunching up in surprise. "Wait, what? Fake? As in—?"

"Not real," I finish for her, feeling the weight of it settle over me as I admit it out loud. "We're not really married. I mean, legally we are, but that's all. It's just…it was supposed to be a business arrangement. Something to help him out with his trust fund and to give me financial support for my music. Nothing more."

Tish leans in closer, her voice low but curious. "Okay…but that's not what this is about, is it? You're not just freaking out over the 'fake' part, are you?"

I shake my head, feeling my stomach twist. "No. That's the problem. I didn't expect to…feel anything. But now I do. I'm starting to have real feelings for him, and I don't know what to do about it."

Tish watches me carefully, waiting for me to go on. I take a deep breath, trying to put the jumble of emotions into words.

"It's his family," I confess, glancing toward the bathroom again just to be sure. "They're controlling, manipulative. His father is constantly pulling the strings, threatening to take away the trust fund if Ethan doesn't fall in line. I don't know how to handle that. I didn't sign up to get involved in his family's mess, but now…it's like I'm stuck in the middle of it."

I don't mention that his family is responsible for tearing my family apart by framing my brother for a crime he didn't commit…that feels too heavy, even for someone like Porita.

She lets out a soft whistle, shaking her head. "Damn, that's rough. And you haven't told him how you feel?"

I shake my head again, frustration bubbling up inside me. "No. I can't. I don't even know how to start that conversation. What if he doesn't feel the same? What if his family finds out about the real reason we're married, and everything falls apart?"

Tish crosses her arms, giving me a firm look. "You're over-thinking this, Arya. Look, if you've got feelings for him, you've got to talk to him about it. I know it's scary, but trust me, it'll only get worse if you keep hiding it."

I bite my lip, torn between wanting to follow her advice and the fear that's been holding me back.

"I know you're right," I admit reluctantly. "But I'm scared. What if it ruins everything?"

Tish's expression softens. "It won't. And even if it does… better to know where you stand than to keep pretending like everything's fine when it's not."

Deep down I know she's right, but the thought of baring my soul to Ethan has me feeling like I'm on the edge of a cliff.

"Okay, I'll talk to him," I finally agree, though the words feel shaky and uncertain. But before I can fully commit, panic flares up in my chest again. "Wait…I can't. Not in the car all the way to Nashville. That'll be a disaster. What if we have this huge argument and I'm stuck in a car with him for hours?"

Tish rolls her eyes, amused. "You're such a chicken."

"Please," I beg, grabbing her arm. "Come with us. Just ride with us to Nashville. That way, I won't have to carry the conversation the whole way, and if things go south, you'll be there to…diffuse it or something."

Tish raises an eyebrow, clearly trying to hold back a laugh. "You're really dragging me into this?"

"Yes!" I say, desperate. "Please, Tish. I'll owe you big time."

She gives me a long, considering look before letting out a dramatic sigh. "Fine. I'll come, but only because it's cheaper than a bus ticket, and I'd rather not get stuck on a Greyhound for five hours."

Relief floods through me, but before I can thank her, she holds up a finger.

"But," she says firmly, "I'm not letting you off the hook. You're going to talk to Ethan. No running away from it, no chickening out. Got it?"

Gratitude and anxiety knot in my stomach. "Got it."

Ethan returns from the restroom a few minutes later. He stops when he sees us, his eyes narrowing just slightly as he glances between me and Tish, clearly sensing something's up.

"What did I miss?" he asks, his voice low and wary.

I swallow, offering him a sheepish smile. "So...um, Tish's going to ride with us to Nashville."

His brow furrows. "Ride with us? As in, in *my* car?"

Tish chimes in with a bright, unbothered grin. "Yep! Arya here thought it would be fun to have some extra company on the ride. Plus, it's cheaper than me grabbing a bus, and I'd rather not endure that nightmare. You don't mind, right?"

Ethan looks taken aback. It's not like we're driving a roomy SUV—his car barely fits the two of us, let alone another person and her luggage.

He exhales slowly, running a hand over his face before turning to Tish. "You've got luggage?"

"Just a small bag," she says, waving it off as if it's no big deal. "I'm low maintenance, promise."

I bite my lip, trying not to laugh at the expression on Ethan's face. He's clearly irritated, but he's holding it together. Barely. His eyes flick to me, and there's this silent exchange between us —he's not thrilled, and I know it, but he's also resigned.

"Fine," he finally mutters, his voice laced with exasperation. "We'll make it work."

Tish claps her hands together, clearly thrilled. "Awesome! I'll grab my stuff, and we'll be good to go."

As she skips off to gather her things, I turn to Ethan and give him another guilty grin.

"I'll make it up to you," I promise him.

"I swear, Arya," he mutters, rubbing the back of his neck, "I leave you alone for ten minutes, and I come back to this."

I can't help but laugh a little. "She's fun!"

Ethan huffs out a breath, shaking his head. "I'm never leaving you alone in a bar again. Ever."

Chapter Fifteen

ARYA

THE CAR RIDE to Nashville is a strange mix of awkward silence and forced conversation, with Tish filling in the gaps whenever things get too tense. I'm grateful for her, really—I don't know what I would've done if it had just been me and Ethan in that car, the weight of everything unspoken hanging between us like a fog. Still, even with Tish there, tension simmers beneath the surface. Tish glances at me in the rearview mirror now and then, her arched brow a clear sign to get on with my conversation with Ethan, but I don't. I can't. I'm still too anxious.

By the time we reach Nashville, I'm more than ready to get out of the car and breathe in some fresh air. The city greets us with its familiar buzz—the hum of traffic, the distant sounds of live music drifting from every corner, and the energy that only Nashville can offer. It's like a heartbeat, constant and steady, and I find myself calming as we pull up to the curb.

Ethan parks and turns off the engine. He doesn't look at me right away, but I can see the strain in his jaw, the way his hands grip the steering wheel like he's holding onto more than just the car. Tish is the first to break the silence, popping open her door and slinging her bag over her shoulder.

"Well, this is my stop," she says brightly, always the one to lighten the mood. "Thanks for the ride, guys. I'll catch you later, Arya. Don't forget what we talked about." She shoots me a knowing look before disappearing into the crowd.

I force a smile, nodding as I watch her go, but inside, there's a heaviness I can't shake. As soon as Tish's gone, the air between Ethan and me thickens again. He finally turns to me, his eyes searching mine, and I think he's going to say something about the conversation we still haven't had.

But instead, he sighs and runs a hand through his hair.

"Listen, I've got to handle something with Jesse," he says, his tone tense. "He's going to send me the trust fund documents behind Dad's back, but I need to talk to him alone. It'll take a few hours so you'll have to go to your two coffee shop gigs alone this afternoon."

My stomach twists slightly as I open the car door and get out. "Okay."

"Be careful," he adds, his voice softening. "I'll be back as soon as I can. Just don't do anything reckless, alright?"

I scoff lightly, rolling my eyes. "I've been taking care of myself long before you came along, Ethan. I'll be fine."

He gives me a long look, and something flickers in his expression—something like worry. Before I can figure it out, he nods and pulls away from the curb, disappearing into the flow of traffic.

As I stand there, watching his car fade into the distance, a strange feeling settles over me. I've gotten used to him being around—his presence, his protectiveness, the way he always steps in, even when I don't ask him to. And now, with him gone, there's this pull in my chest, a small ache that catches me off guard. I miss him. Which is ridiculous because I've always prided myself on being independent, on not needing anyone to look out for me. But still, the feeling is there, gnawing at me.

Shaking it off, I clutch my violin case tighter and head toward my first engagement for the day. I've got two coffee shop gigs lined up, back-to-back, then a nightclub later, and I can't afford to get distracted by thoughts of Ethan. Like I told him, I'm more than capable of taking care of myself.

The first coffee shop is cozy, with dim lighting and the smell of freshly brewed espresso filling the air. I set up in the corner, tuning my violin while a handful of customers mill about, some paying attention, others lost in their own conversations. When I start my performance, I lose myself in the music, my bow gliding across the strings as I play through my set, the familiar rhythm soothing the unease that's been sitting in my chest all morning.

By the time I finish, there's a small crowd gathered, clapping politely. I smile, thanking them before packing up and heading to the next spot. The second coffee shop is busier, with people crammed into every available seat. The energy is different—more alive, more chaotic—but it's the kind of chaos I can handle. I play through the noise, letting the music take over until there's nothing but the notes and the steady hum of the city around me.

The day's starting to catch up with me, exhaustion settling in. But I've got one more gig lined up for the night—a nightclub downtown, where the energy is bound to be even higher and where I'll be able to put on a full show with wilder music and dancing.

The nightclub has a heavy thrum of bass that hits me the second I walk through the door. It's dark and packed with people—exactly the kind of scene where I can lose myself in the music. As I make my way toward the small stage, my eyes scan the crowd, looking for one face that's not there.

Still no sign of Ethan.

I try not to let the disappointment settle in, but it's there, gnawing at the back of my mind. He said he'd be back by now, or at least close to it. I take a deep breath, pushing it down. I've got a show to get through, and I can't afford to let my headspace get too tangled in thoughts of him. I head backstage to the small, cramped green room and start setting up. The stage crew is already busy prepping the lights and sound, and I move to the side, tuning my violin, running through my set list in my head. This gig is important—Nashville is important—and I can't let my emotions mess this up.

Just as I'm about to head out for a sound check, I hear a familiar voice behind me.

"Hey, superstar."

I turn to see Tish leaning against the doorframe, a grin on her face. She looks completely at ease, like she's been in a thousand places like this before, and maybe she has. I smile, glad to see a friendly face.

"You came!"

"Of course. I'm not gonna miss your big Nashville debut." She steps inside, glancing around the cramped green room. "Place has a vibe, huh?"

I laugh. "Yeah, it's something."

She walks over to me, glancing at my set list. "You nervous?"

"A little," I admit, my fingers fiddling with the bow in my hand. "But I think I'll be okay."

"You'll do great," she says, her tone confident. Then, a spark of mischief lights up her eyes. "You know…I've been dying to do another song with you. What do you say we do one tonight?"

I blink, surprised, but excitement bubbles up. "Really? You want to?"

"Absolutely," she grins. "I've got a killer harmony for 'Losing Ground' if you're down for it."

"Yeah. Let's do it."

The sound check goes smoothly, and soon, it's showtime. As I step onto the stage, the lights hit me, and the hum of the crowd fills my ears. I push everything else aside—Ethan, the complicated mess of feelings I've been trying to ignore, the robbery—and let the music take over.

I move through the first few songs with ease, the audience swaying with the rhythm, and when it's time for "Losing Ground," I call Tish up to join me. Her voice blends effortlessly with mine, the harmonies filling the room in a way that feels natural. The crowd loves it, and I feel the high of the performance—like everything is falling into place, at least on the stage.

When the set's over, the applause ringing in my ears, we head backstage and into the green room. I collapse onto the small couch, my body buzzing with adrenaline, and Tish sits next to me, wiping sweat from her brow.

"You killed it out there," she says, grinning as she hands me a bottle of water.

"So did you," I reply, taking a long sip. "That was incredible. Thanks for jumping in."

"Anytime." Tish winks. " Let's go get a drink to celebrate how amazing we both are.

———

Sitting with Tish, I'm still buzzing from the performance, but underneath the adrenaline is a growing knot of worry. I haven't seen Ethan since he left to handle whatever he needed to with Jesse, and as the minutes stretch into hours, the uneasy feeling gnawing at me gets harder to ignore.

I take another sip of my drink, the ice clinking softly in the glass, but it does nothing to quiet the anxious voice in my head. Where is he? What's taking so long?

"You alright?" Tish asks, noticing my restless glances toward the door.

I force a smile, shrugging. "Yeah, just...I don't know. Haven't heard from Ethan. It's not like him to be gone this long."

She gives me a sympathetic look but doesn't press further. I pull out my phone and send him a quick text asking where he is. No response. The knot tightens.

"Alright," I mutter to myself. "I'm just gonna find him."

I get the address for the hotel we booked for the night and call an Uber. Tish offers to come with me, but I wave her off, telling her I'll be fine. Before we say goodbye, she tells me she'll be in New York for a few days to visit her sister. Her time in the city overlaps with mine, so she'll be at my audition to cheer me on. I thank her and tell her I'll look forward to having her there, but I'm distracted by my worry for Ethan. As I step outside, the humid Nashville night wraps around me, thick and heavy, making the air feel like it's pressing down on my skin. It's warm, even this late, and the sounds of the city buzz in the background.

The ride to the hotel is short, and when I arrive, I step out onto the quiet street, scanning the front parking lot for any sign of Ethan. Nothing. I head inside, my stomach twisting when I ask at the front desk, and the clerk tells me Ethan hasn't checked in yet.

Okay, now I'm *really* worried.

I step outside and dial his number. The phone rings twice before I hear it—the unmistakable sound of his ringtone coming from somewhere nearby. I turn, following the sound around the corner of the building, and there he is, sitting on a curb in front of his car in the side parking lot, his elbows resting on his knees, head bowed like the weight of the world is on his shoulders.

The knot in my chest tightens as I walk over, my footsteps quiet on the asphalt. I don't say anything at first, just take a seat next to him on the curb. The air is thick with humidity, and the distant hum of cars driving by feels far away, like we're sitting in our own little bubble of silence.

For a long time, neither of us speaks. The silence stretches, but it's not uncomfortable—more like he's trying to gather himself, to figure out how to say whatever's on his mind. I steal a glance at him, the soft glow of the streetlights casting shadows over his face. He looks exhausted, worn down in a way that goes deeper than just physical tiredness.

Eventually, he breaks the silence, his voice low and rough. "What's it like?"

I blink, confused. "What do you mean?"

He exhales, staring down at his hands. "What's it like being able to choose your own path? To not have your family pressuring you with their expectations that you don't feel like you can ever escape?"

I let his words sink in, and suddenly, I understand. This isn't just about his father or the trust fund. It's about everything—about the expectations, the control, the weight of always being under someone else's thumb.

I let out a soft breath, leaning on my hands and looking up at the stars barely visible through the hazy night sky. "I wish I could say I know what that's like. But honestly? I have no idea. I don't have any family, other than my brother."

He glances over at me, surprised, but I keep my gaze on the sky, my voice quieter now. "I can empathize with feeling like you have no control over your own life. My brother was arrested for something he didn't do. I was put into the foster system, where I had no control of anything. I've never had to fit anyone's expectations because no one expected anything of me. If they didn't like me, I was moved to a new home. That was it."

He's quiet, processing what I said, and then he leans next to me, his head tilted up toward the sky.

"Yeah. That's exactly it. People dictating what you can and can't do with your life. Making decisions for you, without bothering to ask what it is you actually want. Even Jesse's stuck in the middle of it. And it's like I don't even know what I'm fighting for anymore."

His face illuminated in the soft light. This is the most open I've seen him in a while, and I can feel something shift between us—like the walls we've both been keeping up are starting to crumble.

"What do *you* want, Ethan?" I ask softly. "Forget your dad, forget the trust fund. What do *you* want for your life?"

He's quiet again, his brow furrowing like he's never really thought about it...and I'm starting to wonder if he ever really has.

SITTING ON THE CURB, my elbows resting on my knees, I let out a long breath, staring at the asphalt. The warm, humid air presses down on me, making everything feel heavier; thoughts, feelings, all of it. Arya's question buzzes in my ears, and coming up with an answer that doesn't pathetic is hard.

In the end, nothing comes to mind but the truth.

"I haven't thought about it beyond getting the trust fund back," I admit, the words tasting bitter in my mouth. "It's so stupid, isn't it? All this work to get that money, and I don't even know what I'm going to do with it once I get it."

The weight of the admission settles between us. I've never told anyone that before. Whenever anyone asked me what I wanted to do once I had my trust, I'd dodge the question. I didn't want people to look down their noses at me because I don't have a solid plan in place. No one needs to judge me for not thinking things through.

Arya sits next to me quietly, not saying anything, just letting me talk. It's strange, this vulnerability. I'm not used to spilling my guts like this, but with her, it feels almost…natural.

"I always thought once I had the money, I could break free from my father, do what I wanted. Now that I'm so close to it,

I'm realizing I have no idea what comes next. I don't have a plan...I don't even know what I'm good at other than pissing my family off."

She's watching me with those soft, understanding eyes of hers when I glance over. It throws me off, the way she looks at me—not with judgment or pity, but with this quiet patience, like she's waiting for me to figure it out for myself. I'm so used to my father's glares of disapproval or impatience whenever I've tried to talk about my future. I stare back at her, feeling truly seen for the first time. It's kind of strange, not having to defend myself, and I experience a rush of appreciation and gratitude toward her for being so accepting and under-standing.

"You're focused," I say, suddenly. "You work hard. You have this clear purpose, this drive, and you just go after it. No hesita-tion. That's what I admire about you, Arya. You've got some-thing you're chasing, and it's real. You know what you want, and that's...that's all I want. A purpose."

Her expression softens. "Ethan, there's a lot about you that I admire too."

My heart hammers at the sincerity in her voice. No one has ever said they admire me before.

"What?"

She shifts on the curb, turning slightly to face me. "You might not see it, but you're intuitive. You're perceptive in a way most people aren't. You pick up on things—about people, about situations—that others miss. And you care. You act like you don't sometimes, like you're cold or distant, but you've been taking care of me even though you really have no obligation to do so from our agreement. That means something, Ethan."

"Nobody takes me seriously," I say quietly, still trying to process what she's telling me. "I'm the playboy with no future. No direction. I'm the guy you come to when you're looking for a good time...but beyond that, I'm not worth a lot to people, especially my father."

She shakes her head. "You're not just that, Ethan. You don't give yourself enough credit."

No one's ever looked at me this way, with this level of insight. The fact that a woman like her—someone so bright, so full of life—sees this potential in me messes with my head. She's not just someone who works hard for what she wants; she's someone who *believes* in people. In me.

"What makes you think there's more to me than what everyone else sees?"

Arya smiles, that soft, knowing smile that makes my chest tighten.

"Because I pay attention," she says simply. "I see that you're capable of so much more than you believe. You're not your father, Ethan, and you're not bound by his expectations. You can be whatever you want to be."

Her words settle over me, and I feel a surge of optimism and motivation for the first time in a long time. Maybe she's right. Maybe I've been so focused on the wrong things that I haven't let myself think about who I really want to be.

The tension in my chest eases just a little.

"You make it sound so simple," I say, a half-smile tugging at my lips.

She laughs softly, nudging me with her shoulder. "It's not simple, but it's worth figuring out."

I gaze at her, and my heart starts racing. I want to kiss her. Take her up to our hotel room and strip her naked and pleasure her all night long. Reaching up, I brush my fingers along her cheek, and she leans into my touch. Slowly, I lean in toward her, but just before my lips touch hers, my phone buzzes in my pocket.

"Damn it, give me just a sec," I hiss, but I pull it out and glance at the screen—it's a new email from Jesse.

My heart kicks up a notch. It's the one I've been waiting for: confirmation that I'm now in full possession of my trust fund.

After spending the day going back and forth with Jesse,

filling out paperwork and consulting legal counsel over the phone, it's finally done. I'm finally free. Jesse sent me electronic copies of everything, and I see he's also CC'd the family's accountant, Gerald, on the email as well. I stare at the screen, the realization slowly sinking in. I've been chasing this for so long, it almost doesn't feel real.

"What is it?" she asks and I glance up at her.

"My brother," I say, my voice soft with relief. "The trust should be all mine now."

A bright smile curls her lips, lighting up her face. "That's fantastic! You've finally got your money. You must be so relieved."

"Yeah…definitely." I am, right?

But then, like a punch to the gut, the thought creeps in: this means Arya and I can get out of this marriage sooner than expected. We'll be able to walk away from this arrangement clean, no strings attached.

That doesn't bring the relief I thought it would. In fact, it leaves me feeling…anxious. My stomach twists and the urge to wrap my arms around Arya and never let her go sweeps through me. I push the feeling down, refusing to linger on it. This was the plan all along, right? We help each other out, and when it's over, we go our separate ways. No mess. No complications. So why does the idea of her walking away feel like a loss?

I slide the phone back into my pocket, stealing a glance at Arya. She's looking up at the sky, her expression soft and peaceful, but there's a hint of something lingering behind her eyes. This tour has been everything for her—her shot at making a name for herself, at getting closer to the dream she's been chasing for so long, but now, with the tour coming to an end, I can see the weight of what comes next pressing down on her.

New York and her audition. She's so close to getting everything she's wanted, and I want to do whatever I can to help her. Her success is important to me now. Seeing her pour her heart and soul into her music and truly love what she's doing is something I haven't witnessed first hand before. My siblings don't love their jobs. They all work for my dad in one way or another, but they do it out of a sense of obligation and not because they're passionate about what they do.

I don't want to be like them. I never have. Instead, I want to be like Arya.

I lean back on my hands, thinking of how I can help her. We have a few days until the audition, and if she has too much down time, she might start stressing out and that could affect her playing. Is there something I can do to distract her and help her stay relaxed in the meantime?

Maybe even get her to have some fun and let her hair down? An idea hits me all at once—Vegas. A crazy trip, something spontaneous and fun. I can show her a good time there, shower her in luxury and spoil her in a way no one ever has.

Plus, it would mean spending more time with her before ending our arrangement, and I'm not ready to walk away from her. This way I can be a little greedy.

The trip would also be something that would piss off my father to no end. He's always hated Vegas, hated everything it stands for: indulgence, risk, chaos. And let's face it—what better way to stick it to him than to show up at one of the flashiest resorts in the city and have the time of our lives?

I smirk at the thought, already imagining the look on his face when he finds out. I turn to Arya.

"Hey," I say, nudging her lightly. She glances over, her expression curious.

"What?" she asks.

"You ever been to a fancy resort or casino?" I ask, keeping my tone casual.

She shakes her head, her brow furrowing in confusion. "No, why?"

"Well," I drawl, leaning in a little, "how do you feel about Vegas? We've got some time before your audition in New York, so why not make a detour? We could stay at one of the best resorts, hit the casinos, maybe even see a show. Go all out."

Her eyes widen, and she looks like she's not sure whether to laugh or take me seriously.

"Vegas?" she repeats, looking baffled.

"Yeah," I say, warming to the idea more and more as I talk. "I mean, think about it. The tour's over, and before you dive headfirst into the chaos of New York, why not blow off some steam? Do something completely different, something fun. I'll charter us a flight so we can get there and then to New York with time to spare."

She laughs then, the sound light and surprised, and it's exactly what I wanted to hear. "You really want to go to Vegas? Just out of the blue?"

I shrug, grinning. "I want to see you have some fun. You've been working nonstop, and you deserve to cut loose."

She bites her lip, her eyes sparkling with excitement now. "I don't know, Ethan. Vegas seems a bit...wild."

I chuckle. "Exactly. That's the point. What do you say?"

She hesitates but then her smile grows, and she nods. "Alright, Vegas. Let's do it."

I grin, feeling a surge of adrenaline. Maybe it's the spontaneity of it, or maybe it's the fact that this is a chance for us to have some real fun—no plans, no stress, just the two of us letting loose. Together.

Vegas, here we come.

Chapter Seventeen

ARYA

LEANING BACK in the plush seat, my gaze drifts out the window as the clouds roll by beneath us. The hum of the private plane is steady and soothing, the kind of sound that should lull me into complete relaxation, but my thoughts are too scattered for that. The complimentary lunch was nice, and the coffee—well, it's the best cup I've had in a long time. Everything feels surreal, like I've stepped into someone else's life.

A private plane. Who would've thought? Certainly not me. I'm used to crowded buses, economy flights, and scraping by to make sure I can get from one gig to the next. Now, here I am, sipping hot coffee with the clouds beneath me. It's strange, but I can't say I hate it.

Ethan is dozing in the seat beside me, his head tipped back slightly, his breathing slow and even. His strong profile is softened in sleep, and I just watch him, trying to make sense of the tangled knot of feelings twisting around inside me.

This man, this complex, maddening, strong-willed man, has somehow worked his way under my skin. I didn't expect it. I didn't plan for it, but here we are.

When I think about the conversation we had last night and how vulnerable he was with me, it makes my chest ache. I wanted to hold him and kiss him to banish the doubts and frustrations he holds onto. It breaks my heart that he can't see how talented and so full of potential he is.

My eyes linger on the way his brow furrows, even in sleep, like he's carrying some invisible weight that never really leaves him. His family's expectations, no doubt. Fuck them. They don't see him for who he really is and that's their loss. He's defended me, looked out for me, and believed me when no one else ever has.

It surprises me how much that matters to me, how much I appreciate it. It reminds me of Lou, before everything went wrong. Lou had that same fierce protectiveness, and I didn't realize just how much I missed that. But Lou's gone and Ethan's here, stepping in when I least expected it, making me feel safe in a way I haven't felt in a long time.

Looking out the window again, the clouds shift and swirl below. I'm nervous about my audition, and overwhelmed by my desire for Ethan. Maybe this impromptu trip to Vegas is just what I need. I can relax and enjoy myself for the next few days and not think about anything but me and Ethan.

Sighing, I pull my phone out and check my email using the plane's wifi. I freeze when I see that I have a new message from the Carnegie Hall orchestra. What could they be reaching out about? Oh, no…they haven't canceled my audition, have they?

Heart racing, I open the email and quickly scan through it.

Dear Miss Jones,
We hope this message finds you well. Due to unforeseen circumstances, we have to reschedule your audition, as one of our directors is no longer able to attend on the 14th. Since you have already planned on being in the city a few days before your audition, we have moved your time slot to 2:00 PM on the 13th. We are sorry for any inconvenience this may cause, and if you are no longer able to make the audition, we can always keep you in mind for next year's open call.

My eyes linger on that last line...*keep you in mind for next year's open call.*

I'd have to wait another whole year? No, no, no, no, no...I can't do that! I put everything on the line for this chance, and now what am I doing? Flying off to Vegas like I'm someone who can afford to risk throwing all my hard work awake?

Panic settling in, I reach over and grab Ethan's shoulder, shaking him.

"Ethan! Ethan, wake up!"

Blinking, he opens his eyes and looks at me with a confused frown.

"What is it?" he asks, his voice rough from sleep. "Are we crashing?"

"No," I answer, exasperated. "The orchestra moved my audition up to the thirteenth. That's only two days from now! We can't go to Vegas. We need to go to New York..."

"Hey, hey, hey, it's okay," he assures me, sitting up and reaching over to grab hold of my hand. He gives it a gentle squeeze. "Don't worry. I'm not going to do anything to put your audition at risk."

"Are you sure we have time?" I ask in a small voice. "I don't want to risk anything happening to keep us from getting there in time."

"Arya, look at me." He stares into my eyes and I can't seem to tear my gaze from his. "I'm going to take care of you. We'll get there on time, I promise."

He smiles softly and leans in and presses his lips to mine in a gentle kiss. He's tender and slow, teasing me until my heart pounds. This isn't like any other kiss we've shared. This one is more intimate...more familiar.

Everything else fades away. The warmth of his hand on my cheek as he cups it, the steady rhythm of his breath, the way he pulls me closer—it all wraps around me like a cocoon. My heart races, the kiss deepening as I lose myself in him. His tongue slides against mine, promising more, and heat floods between my legs.

He devours my mouth like he can't get enough. Even when his lips are hard and hungry, there's a tenderness in his touch, as if I'm something precious that he wants to handle with care. It makes my heart race and my blood sizzle.

The pilot's voice crackles over the intercom. "Mr. Cavenwell, we are beginning our descent into Las Vegas. Please prepare for landing."

The timing couldn't be worse. Disappointed by the interruption, I pull back, both of us breathing a little heavier than before. There's a brief moment where we just stare at each other, caught in the lingering electricity sparking between us. Ethan smirks, his thumb brushing lightly across my cheek before he sits back with a sigh.

"Damn, things were just getting good," he says, his voice low and teasing.

My blood is heated and it's all I can do not to drag his mouth back to mine. *Be good, Arya.* If I'm very lucky, there will be more of that later…

To try and take my mind off my unsatisfied desire, I grab my phone and shoot Tish a text to let her know the audition is a day earlier than originally planned.

The plane descends through the clouds, and soon, the bright lights of the Las Vegas skyline come into view. It's like nothing I've ever seen before—neon lights stretching as far as the eye can see, glittering buildings rising against the dark desert sky. The excitement bubbling up in my chest is impossible to ignore. What would it be like coming to this city to play? To stand on one of the many famous stages throughout the strip and have people lining up to get inside for my show? It would be dazzling, I have no doubt. Maybe someday I'll actually get to see that vision become reality.

This is the Entertainment Capital of the World, and I'm about to dive right into the heart of it.

When we land, it's all a blur of luxury. A sleek black limo is waiting for us as soon as we step off the plane, the driver holding the door open as we slip inside. Ethan slides in next to me, and as the limo glides through the city streets, I can't help but stare out the window in awe. The lights, the people, the energy—it's all so alive, so electric.

"First stop," Ethan says, his hand resting casually on my knee, "we're catching a show. Thought you might like it."

"Really?" I ask, unable to keep my excitement out of my voice.

He nods. "Cirque du Soleil. Have you ever seen one of their shows?"

Shaking my head, I answer, "No, never, but I've always wanted to."

"Then you're in for a treat."

A few minutes later, we arrive at the resort where the show is in residence. Ethan holds my hand as we make our way into the cavernous theater and find our seats; a private balcony with a view of the entire stage. The lights dim, and the hum of excited chatter fades to a low murmur as the stage comes alive with a soft, ethereal glow. I sit on the edge of my seat, my heart fluttering in anticipation

The music starts, soft at first, delicate, like the tinkling of distant chimes. It builds, layer by layer, swelling into a haunting melody that seems to fill the entire space. My eyes are glued to the stage, where shadows begin to move in sync with the music, the performers emerging from the darkness.

And then, suddenly, it all bursts into color.

Dancers swirl onto the stage, their movements impossibly fluid, like they're made of water and air. Every step, every leap, every spin is perfectly timed, and I can't look away. Their costumes shimmer under the lights—vibrant blues, golds, and reds, catching every flicker of movement as they twist and twirl through the air. It's like watching a living, breathing painting unfold before my eyes, each stroke more breathtaking than the last.

Above the stage, acrobats soar through the air, their bodies twisting and spinning with such grace it feels like they're defying gravity. They catch ropes, swing from trapezes, and flip through the air in perfect synchronization. My breath catches in my throat as one performer leaps from a towering platform, twisting in midair before landing seamlessly in another performer's arms. How do they make it look so effortless?

The stage itself is constantly shifting—one moment, it's a mystical forest, the next, a deep, swirling ocean. Each scene is crafted so perfectly, so meticulously, that it feels like I'm being transported to another realm with every transition. The lighting, the set design, the music—it's all so immersive, pulling me deeper and deeper into their world.

A contortionist takes the stage next, her body bending in ways I didn't think were possible. Every move she makes is slow, deliberate, yet filled with such intensity. The audience is silent, completely mesmerized, and I realize I've been holding my breath, completely absorbed in the performance.

It's the final act that really takes my breath away, though. The lights dim once more, and all eyes are drawn to the massive aerial silk hanging from the ceiling. A performer climbs it with ease, her body twisting and wrapping in the silk until she's high above the stage. The music shifts, growing darker, more intense, and she begins to descend, twirling and spinning with breath-taking speed, the fabric unraveling with her movements. Each drop is more daring than the last. It's thrilling and terrifying all at once.

I'm utterly captivated.

By the time the final note of music fades and the lights come back up, I'm left breathless, my heart pounding in my chest. The performers take their bows, the audience erupts into applause, and I find myself clapping so hard my hands hurt. I don't know how to describe it. It wasn't just a show. It was an experience, an emotional rollercoaster wrapped in color, music, and impossible feats of strength and grace. There's this sense of wonder still clinging to me, like I've been touched by something magical, something beyond the everyday. I'm left buzzing, my mind filled with inspiration, my soul full of light.

It's not just the spectacle—it's the artistry, the way they moved, the emotions they conveyed without words. It reminds me why I love performing, why I've fought so hard for my music. I want to capture this feeling, this sense of magic, and carry it with me, weave it into every note I play, every stage I step onto.

As we leave the theater, my head is still spinning, the colors and sounds of Cirque du Soleil playing on a loop in my mind. I feel more alive, more inspired than I have in a long time. This is what I live for. The beauty, the intensity, the connection. And now, I want more than ever to chase after that magic, to create something just as breathtaking in my own way.

Ethan watches me, a wide smile curling his lips as we make our way to the limo.

"You look like you're on cloud nine," he says, sliding in beside me as we settle into the plush seats.

"I am," I admit, still glowing from the experience. "That was incredible. Everything about it—the music, the way they moved, the way it all came together. It was like magic."

He chuckles, his hand finding mine again and giving it a gentle squeeze. "I knew you'd love it."

As the limo glides through the streets of Vegas, taking us to our hotel, I can't stop smiling. The city feels like it's alive, pulsing with possibility, and I feel like I'm a part of it. It's more than just the glitz and glam, more than the lights and the luxury. It's the way this place makes me feel—like anything is possible, like my dreams are right there, within reach.

I turn my gaze to Ethan and feel overwhelmed with gratitude toward him. He brought me here. He gave me this. Even though he didn't have to, instead of going to New York and spending the next couple days stressing over the audition, Ethan chose to bring me here and distract me with fun and attention. Spoiling me like I'm really his wife.

My heart flips in my chest at the thought. What would it be like to really spend my life with this man? To have him doting on me and showering me with affection on a daily basis?

It almost seems like a fairy tale...and I can't help but wish that it could be my reality.

I lean my head against Ethan's shoulder and let out a happy sigh, my worries from early completely forgotten as I revel in the life pulsing in the city around us, and the warmth of the man sitting next to me, his hand wrapped comfortably around mine. Maybe this is a fairy tale, and soon enough I'll have to go back to the real world without Ethan by my side. For now, though, I'm going to soak up every moment I can with this man.

Chapter Eighteen

ETHAN

THE LIMO GLIDES to a smooth stop in front Bellagio, the neon lights from the marquee above casting a colorful glow over Arya as she sits beside me, still buzzing with excitement from the show. I glance over at her, and I can't help but feel enchanted. Her eyes are wide as she takes in everything around her. I've seen her light up before, but here, in Vegas, she's a whole different kind of magic.

It hits me, suddenly, how much I love being the one who gets to show her all of this. The billionaire life. The luxury, the excitement, the things most people never get to experience. It makes me feel—hell, I don't know—like the greatest guy in the world. Especially when she's this happy, this alive. And when she looks this damn good while doing it? It's almost too much.

She's beautiful when she's in her element on stage, but when she's excited like this? When she's seeing something new, something extraordinary? It's so fucking hot I've got a semi just watching her. I want her to look at *me* like that. I want to put that wonder in her eyes, make that same excitement hum through her whole body as I light her up with my hands, my mouth, my cock. Would it be too gauche for Vegas to throw her over my shoulder and sprint through the hotel lobby straight up to our room? I don't think I can keep my hands to myself for the time it takes to check in.

As we step out of the limo and into the bright, bustling lobby of the hotel, I'm already making plans. Flowers. Definitely. I'll have a bouquet sent up to the room—roses, or maybe something more exotic. Maybe I'll order something lacy for her, too. Something sexy.

Though, that might be more for me than for her.

Inside the Bellagio, it's all marble floors, towering ceilings, and chandeliers dripping with glass and light. The Bellagio doesn't just show off wealth—it flaunts it. Every detail, from the decor to the service, is designed to make you feel like you've stepped into a different world, a world where anything is possible if you have enough money.

The lobby stretches out like a casino version of paradise. Giant flower displays, expensive artwork on the walls—everything polished to perfection. The noise from the casino floor hums in the distance, the familiar sounds of slot machines chiming and cards being shuffled mixing with the low murmur of voices. It's almost hypnotic.

I guide her toward the front desk with a hand on her lower back. A few more inches and I could be cupping her luscious ass.

Before we even make it to the concierge, Arya darts off in the direction of the hotel gift shop.

"I'll be right back!" she calls, waving me on as she hurries away.

I chuckle under my breath, shaking my head. She's like a whirlwind. I keep one eye on her as she disappears into the shop while I step up to the desk to check in.

"Good evening, Mr. Cavenwell," the concierge greets me with a practiced smile. Her dark hair is pulled back into a sleek, neat bun, not a strand out of place, giving her a polished, almost regal appearance. She's wearing the hotel's tailored uniform, a crisp navy blazer with gold buttons, the sharp lines of her attire highlighting her attention to detail. "Welcome to the Bellagio. I see you've reserved the penthouse suite for two nights."

"Yeah," I say, sliding my credit card across the counter. "Looking forward to it."

The concierge takes my card, running it through the system with a calm efficiency, but then her smile falters. She frowns slightly, trying again.

"I'm terribly sorry, Mr. Cavenwell, but it seems your card has been declined. Would you happen to have another form of payment?"

What?

I blink, momentarily stunned. My card's never been declined before. Ever. I hand her another card, frowning now.

"Try this one."

She swipes it again, her expression turning apologetic. "I'm sorry, sir. This one's also been declined."

Irritation simmers just beneath my skin. There's no way this is happening right now. I glance at the gift shop where Arya is still browsing. Great. I give the concierge one last card.

"Here, try this."

But when that one declines, too, I know something's wrong.

"Give me a moment," I tell the woman.

I step off to the side, trying to keep my cool, but inside I'm fuming. This doesn't just happen. Not to me. I dial the family's accountant, Gerald, my jaw clenched as I listen to the rings. Dad pays him a hefty retainer so I know he'll answer.

"Mr. Cavenwell," Gerald finally answers. "It's a little late, isn't it?"

I take a deep breath, trying to keep my voice steady. "Apologies. All of my cards just got declined at the Bellagio in Vegas. I need to know what's going on."

"Give me a moment." There's silence on the other end when he puts me on hold—probably because I woke him out of a dead sleep and he's nowhere near a computer. That moment stretches into what feels like three hours while I wait, stewing in my anger. There's no fucking way this is "just happened."

Gerald comes back on and I hear the click of keyboard keys as he pulls up my information. "It seems there's been a hold placed on all of your accounts by the primary trustee of your trust."

Rage flares hot in my chest. Of course. *Of course*, it's Dad.

"What's the reason for the hold?" I ask, even though I already know the answer.

Gerald hesitates, but eventually, he reads it off. "Um, I apologize Mr. Cavenwell, but the exact message given was, 'My son is clearly in the power of a gold-digger.'"

The words hit me like a slap in the face. My hand tightens around my phone as I step further away from the front desk, trying to calm the fire building inside me.

Apparently, Dad still has a few hands to play.

I grit my teeth, barely keeping my voice in check as I say, "Turn the cards back on. Now."

"I'm afraid I'll need authorization from the primary—"

"It's *my* money," I snap, cutting him off. "And these are my credit cards. You've received the paperwork from Jesse—I have primary control over the trust now. I don't care what my father says. I want the hold lifted. Now."

There's a long pause on the other end, but I don't back down. I can't. The last thing I'm going to do is let my father ruin this night, ruin this trip, ruin whatever the hell it is I'm building with Arya.

Finally, Gerald speaks again. "I'll process the request, Mr. Cavenwell. It may take a few moments for the cards to reset."

"Thank you," I say tightly before hanging up. I let out a long breath, trying to shake off the urge to strangle my father with my bare hands. *There's nothing else he can do,* I remind myself. I control my trust, his hold over me is gone.

Arya's still bustling around in the gift shop. She has no idea what just went down, and I'm glad. She doesn't need to know. Not right now. I want her to remain carefree while we're here.

Returning to the front desk, I tell the concierge, "Everything should be fine now."

She nods. "Very good, Mrs. Cavenwell. I'll run your card again."

As the concierge finishes up the check-in process, I step to the side again and hit Jesse's number in my phone. It rings a few times, and then my brother's groggy voice comes on the line.

"Ethan? It's the middle of the night, man. What's going on?"

"Yeah, well, you can thank our *beloved* father for that." My voice drips with sarcasm. I keep an eye on the gift shop, making sure Arya doesn't catch any of this. "He just had all my cards shut off. Says I'm 'under the influence of a gold-digger.' Can you believe that?"

There's a pause on the other end, and Jesse sighs, clearly trying to wake up and catch up at the same time.

"Jesus, Ethan. He actually did it, huh? You've got to know he's losing it if he's pulling this kind of stunt. But…are you sure Arya's not—"

"No," I cut him off sharply, my tone leaving no room for argument. "Don't even start with that. She's not after the money. She doesn't give a damn about any of it, and I'm done with his paranoia, Jesse. This isn't about her—it's about *him* trying to control me. Again."

Jesse lets out another long breath, and I can hear him shifting, probably sitting up in bed. "Alright, alright. So what do you want me to do?"

I lower my voice, my anger simmering just beneath the surface. "I need you to help me move the trust fund. Now. I want it somewhere Dad can't reach it, and I don't care what it takes. After this stunt? It's personal."

Jesse doesn't argue, which I appreciate. He knows when to

push and when to back off, and tonight, I'm not in the mood for any more pushback.

"Okay," he says, his voice steady. "I'll help but it's going to take a minute. You'll need to log into the account with your computer, and we'll have to change your passwords and set up new secondary authentications. Right now they all go through Dad."

"Fine," I mutter, running a hand through my hair. I glance at the concierge, who's waiting for me to sign something. I quickly scribble my name on the paperwork and hand it back, all while keeping my phone pressed to my ear. "Just tell me what I need to do."

Jesse starts listing off steps, talking me through some of it. My mind is split between the conversation and Arya, who's now heading toward me, a bright smile on her face and a small shopping bag in her hand. I glance at the logo on the bag and feel my breath catch for a second—it's from a lingerie brand.

Well, fuck. That's...distracting.

"Ethan?" Jesse's voice breaks through my thoughts. "Did you hear me? I need you to log into the account as soon as you can."

I shake my head, trying to refocus. "Yeah, yeah. I'll do it when I get to the room. Let me call you back."

I hang up the call before Jesse can say anything else as Arya reaches me, looking positively radiant, her eyes gleaming with excitement from her detour. I flash her a smile, trying to act casual, but my mind is definitely not focused on financial security right now.

"Everything good?" she asks, glancing at my phone with a hint of curiosity.

"Yeah, just handling some stuff with Jesse," I say, holding up the key cards the concierge handed me. "Ready to head up?"

She nods, and we walk across the lobby together, my hand on her back again. I can't stop touching her. I want her close... closer than decency allows as we step into the elevator. I barely stop myself from ravaging her as the doors slide shut. She looks happy but suddenly a little shy so I convince my dick it can wait the three minutes it takes to get to our room.

I glance down and catch sight of that shopping bag in Arya's hands again, though, my dick disagrees. Shit. What delicious little piece of nothing is in that thing?

We reach our floor, and I lead Arya down the hallway to our room. She's smiling as we walk, her energy infectious, and I can't help but feel a surge of pride that I'm the one who gave her this. I'm the one who gets to share all of this with her.

Finally, we reach the door, and I fumble with the key card, opening it and stepping inside. The suite is massive—high ceilings, plush furniture, and a view of the Vegas Strip that takes your breath away. Arya lets out a soft gasp, walking toward the window, and I just drink her in. I know I need to call Jesse, that this shit with my dad is beyond serious, but I let myself picture pinning her naked against those windows and making her beg for it.

What kind of lingerie did she pick? Satin? Lace?

The porter arrives with our bags just then, and my phone buzzes, breaking me from my lust-filled stupor. Jesse. Shit. That rage comes back, the anxiety. After that stunt dad pulled I'm desperate to move my money, putting out of his reach forever

My thoughts must show on my face because Arya gives me a questioning look when I grab my computer bag and pull my laptop out.

"Sorry," I say, trying to act like it's no big deal. "I just need a few minutes. Have to straighten some things out with Jesse." No need for both of us to worry. This trip is about her taking a break from stress and everything about my dad is stress-inducing.

My phone buzzes again. "This might take a little bit. Why don't you relax and get comfortable?"

Arya just flashes me a thumbs up and wanders off toward the bathroom. I can hear her voice faintly as she talks to herself, something about a big tub. Water starts to run. I need to wrap this mess up right the fuck now and get in there.

I answer the call finally. "All right, Jesse, what do I need to do?"

"Log into your account, change who gets notifications about new login attempts, and immediately your password," he instructs. "Once that's done, change the permissions on who can access the account. After that—"

"Hang on, my laptop hasn't even booted up yet."

Jesse sighs like I'm holding him up for prom or something. "Once you're back, we'll set you up with my accountant. You need to stop using Gerald. Who knows what Dad might do to pressure him into giving up your new info."

It doesn't surprise me at all that even Jesse, who does everything our father asks of him, still needs to protect his assets just in case he pisses dad off.

Jesse's voice is still buzzing in my ear as I pull up the account. I glance at the balance, expecting to see the usual. Something's wrong. My eyes narrow as I take in the numbers, my chest tightening.

The balance isn't just low. It's zero.

I blink, my stomach dropping.

"Jesse, what the hell is this?" I snarl, leaning closer to the screen.

"What do you mean?" Jesse sounds confused, and I can hear him shifting on his end of the call.

"I mean the money. The entire trust fund. The balance is zero —it's *gone*. What the hell is going on?"

There's silence on the other end of the line, and I can practically hear Jesse's brain kicking into overdrive as he scrambles to make sense of what I'm telling him. I start clicking through the account details, the transactions stretching back over years, all with the same pattern. Small withdrawals at first that I didn't notice. The withdrawals grew larger and larger within the last few months, though. I haven't been checking the account regularly, assuming the money was just sitting there, untouched while we worked everything out. While I wasn't paying attention, the entire account has been bled dry.

"Dad's been pulling money from the trust," I say, the words barely making it past the tightness in my throat. "It's all gone."

"Gone? Like...everything?"

I run a hand through my hair, my fingers shaking slightly. "Yeah. All of it. Over a series of transactions, he's drained the entire thing."

This was supposed to be my ticket out. My escape. Everything I'd been counting on, the money that would finally let me break free of my father's grip—and it's just...vanished.

"I can't believe he did this." There's a hollowness deep inside of me. It's not just about the money—it's about the realization that my father has been one step ahead this entire time. Here I was, thinking he was just holding the trust over my head, when in reality, he'd taken it all—taken my future.

"Jesse," I say after a long pause, my voice tight. "I'm fucked without this money. What can I do? Can I sue him? This is fucking theft!"

I hear Jesse sigh heavily on the other end, and we're both silent. We've grown up knowing our father wasn't the type to just let us walk away. But this? This is something else.

"Shit," Jesse replies. "You're right, but...suing him? He's Senator Fucking Cavenwell. We need to get a lawyer we can trust. Dad's got a lot of connections and a lot of people in his pocket."

Just like that, the weight of it all crashes down on me. My chance at freedom, at controlling my own life, is gone. Stolen out from under me, and there's nothing I can do to get it back.

Chapter Nineteen

ARYA

THE BUBBLES in the tub feel like heaven against my skin, warm and soft, with the faint scent of lavender filling the air. The tub is so huge, it's like a mini spa. I let out a contented sigh, sinking deeper into the water. I've been thinking about everything that's coming—New York, the audition at Carnegie Hall, and maybe even the chance to finally help my brother. When I land my position with the orchestra, I'll be able to save up money to get a lawyer for Lou's case, and they'll be able to help me find him. It all feels so close, like all my dreams could come true in just a matter of days.

I splash the water a little, smiling to myself as I think about living in New York. The energy, the music, the constant hum of the city—it feels like exactly where I'm meant to be. I close my eyes, letting the warmth of the bath relax me even further. I feel like I'm floating on the high of everything—Vegas, this hotel, me and Ethan…

The door bursts open, and he comes in.

I don't open my eyes at first, just chirp at him happily, "You have to check out this tub! It's like a swimming pool. And the bath oils? They smell amazing!" I gather up the bubbles coyly in my hands, peeking out from under my lashes to see his reaction.

But he doesn't smile. He doesn't even look like he's hearing me. He just sits down heavily with his back against the tub, his shoulders slumped in a way that makes my heart drop. The weight in his posture, the way he's carrying himself—it's like the world just fell on him.

I sit up straighter, the bubbles forgotten as concern rushes through me.

"Ethan?" I ask softly, my voice losing all its playfulness. "What's going on?"

He doesn't answer right away, his hands rubbing over his face before he lets out a long breath. The silence between us feels heavy, and my stomach twists. Finally, he speaks, his voice low and tight.

"The trust fund," he mutters. "It's gone. All of it. My father's been draining it for years, and I just...I didn't see it until now."

The words hit me like a cold wave. Gone? I blink, the reality of what he's saying sinking in. My heart immediately breaks for him. How could his father be so cruel? I knew Jared Cavenwell was a monster, but for him to fuck over his own son like this is awful. Is everyone just a pawn for him to manipulate however he sees fit?

"Oh, Ethan," I whisper, moving closer to him. "I'm so sorry."

He lets out a bitter laugh, leaning his head back against the tub. "Yeah, I don't know what the hell I'm going to do now. I know I need a lawyer, but this was supposed to be my way out. The thought of continuing to have to fight my dad is just... exhausting."

I reach out, resting my hand on his shoulder, and he turns to face me.

"He's not going to win, Ethan," I say, trying to offer him some comfort. "We'll think of something, okay? You're not alone in this."

He's quiet and I can see the defeat written all over his face.

At length, he shrugs, resting his chin on his arms, which he's laid on the edge of the tub.

"I appreciate that, Arya. I really do, but…it would probably be easier just to work for my dad at this point. Wear a suit. Go to board meetings. Pretend I give a fuck about his political career. Otherwise, it'll just be the same thing over and over again. I try to break free, and he finds a way to tighten his hold on me."

The resignation in his voice stirs some protective instinct in me. I don't know that there's much I can do to really help him; I can't even afford a lawyer for Lou right now, and I have no idea how trust funds work.

What I can do is remind Ethan that I'm here. I'm with him. I support him.

That I want him.

"Forget the trust for tonight." I stand up in the tub, blushing as water drips off my naked body. He stares up at me in momentary surprise, but then his eyes darken with clear hunger. I have his full attention now and the power is heady, filling my body with desire even though I feel a little exposed. His eyes track my every movement as I step out of the tub and wrap a towel around me. Damn. Why didn't I bring my lingerie to change into?

Though, if I had, I doubt we'd make it out of the bathroom. I head into the bedroom and he follows me. I grab one of the shopping bags from my spree in the gift shop downstairs.

"I, uh…I actually got you something," I say quietly, glancing over my shoulder at him. I feel nervous, a little afraid that he'll think my gift is cheesy, but when I saw it in the giftshop, I immediately thought of him.

Ethan looks at me, his brow furrowed. "What?"

I take a breath before pulling out a small box and handing it to him.

"It's not much," I tell him. "But the moment I saw it, I knew I had to get it for you."

He opens the box slowly, and when he sees what's inside, he freezes. It's a ring, a simple design with a tiny sunburst etched into the silver. Nothing fancy, but it felt like something that might give him comfort.

"It felt weird being the only one wearing a ring in this whole arrangement," I explain, "but I'm not trying to pressure you or anything like that. I just wanted you to have a reminder that the sunshine always breaks through. Even when things are tough. Even when it feels impossible, good things can happen."

He stares at the ring, and I can't tell what he's thinking. My heart flutters nervously in my chest. Finally, he looks at me, his eyes softer than I've seen them in a while.

"Arya…" he starts, his voice low. "You didn't have to do this."

"I wanted to." And that look in his eyes says I did the right thing. "You're always looking out for me, making sure I'm okay. I just wanted you to have something to remind you that you're not alone. That you've got someone in your corner. Let me be your sunshine."

He's quiet again. He peers back down at the ring, his fingers brushing over the sunburst design. A genuine smile tugs at the corner of his mouth.

"Thank you," he says, his voice barely above a whisper.

I smile back, my heart lighter. "You don't need to thank me, Ethan."

We gaze at each other for several moments before Ethan closes the distance between us. He cups my face in both his hands and pulls me into a hungry kiss. I open my mouth immediately and he sweeps his tongue inside as he grabs hold of the front of my towel and rips it away from my body. I'm naked and still wet from my bath. He's fully clothed and dry, and I want to feel his skin against mine. Grabbing the hem of his shirt, I tug it up, pulling back from the kiss so I can yank it off over his head. Once his chest is bare, I splay my hands across his pecs and press kisses along his throat.

Ethan lets out a low growl before grabbing my ass and lifting me off the floor. I wrap my legs around his waist and he turns to carry me to the bed.

"Ethan," I gasp against his mouth.

"I got you, baby." He sits on the bed with me on his lap and holds me tight as his lips slant over mine.

Moaning, I grip his hair as I return his kiss. My blood is running hot in my veins and I'm getting wet. I can't help myself and grind myself against him.

"Fuck," he growls. "You drive me crazy."

I take his bottom lip between my teeth and give it a playful tug.

Before he can respond, I push against his chest so that he lies on the bed. I want to distract him. Make him forget about anything other than me for just a little while, so I'm taking charge.

"What are you doing?" he asks, his voice rough and husky.

"Just lay back and enjoy," I tell him, moving to settle between his legs. Holding his gaze, I grin as I undo his pants and tug them down his thighs, along with his underwear. His cock springs free, already half-hard. Desire pulses through me at the sight. "My, my, my…someone's eager."

When I wrap my fingers around the base of his shaft, he lets out a hiss of breath and I feel powerful to have this effect over him with just a touch. I drag my tongue along the head before sucking it between my lips.

"Fuck, Arya," he groans.

I lower my head and take him in deeper. Closing my eyes, I savor the taste of him. He gets fully erect, and he's so long and thick, I almost can't fit him all in my mouth. I listen to his moans and growls of pleasure and I feel a rush, knowing I'm the one making him feel so good.

"Hold on," he suddenly orders, and sits up. Confused, I release his cock from my mouth.

"Is it not good?" I ask.

"No, it's great," he assures me, "but I want to lick your pussy while you suck me. Get that sweet ass of yours up here."

I feel a rush of wetness between my legs and I hurry to obey, swinging myself around and straddling his face as he lies down. I'm shivering with excitement as he grips my hips. When he swipes his tongue along my pussy, I whimper and eagerly take him back between my lips.

We move in tandem. As he licks my pussy, I suck his cock, and I'm soon going crazy with pleasure. I take him into my throat as he presses two fingers into my entrance. When I groan around his shaft, he growls against my clit. It's like we're trying to one-up each other. Pleasure each other more intensely with each suck of our lips or drag of our tongues.

Soon, I'm teetering on the edge of my release and I let his cock drop from my mouth again as my body seizes and I cry out as wave after wave of pleasure crashes over me.

Before my orgasm has completely subsided, he moves us again.

"Lie down," he says, his voice husky.

He guides my hips away from his face and I crawl to the middle of the bed and turn onto my back. Ethan looms over me, his eyes blazing with hunger. Pushing my legs apart, he shoves his cock inside me and I cry out in bliss. He catches the sound with his lips, kissing me as he thrusts in and out of me again and again. Wrapping my arms around his shoulders, I cling to him as he pounds me hard and fast.

"You're so fucking perfect," he groans in my ear. "You feel so good. The way you squeeze me…your greedy little pussy can't get enough, can it?"

"I can't get enough," I gasp. "Don't stop…don't stop!"

"Arya!" he roars as he slams into me a final time, his back bowing with the force of his release. As he fills me with his cum,

I go over the edge one more time as the blinding pleasure becomes so intense, it's dancing along the line of pain.

It's as if we're suspended in pleasure, the world disappearing around us as we cling to each other and float through the abyss. I don't want to let him go. There's a part of me that wants to stay like this, wrapped in each other, forever.

Soon enough, we come floating back down to earth. I continue to hold him, burying my face in his neck. The room is silent save for our panting breaths.

"What are you doing to me?" he whispers at length.

Whatever it is, he's doing the same thing to me. I simply cling to him tighter, afraid that if I let him go, he'll slip away from me.

Chapter Twenty

ETHAN

SITTING across from Arya in the private plane the next morning, I can't stop watching her. She's radiant and practically glowing, a literal burst of sunshine as she spreads butter on her toast. I should be focused on solving the mess with the trust fund, but instead, I'm caught up in this feeling that I could get used to this. Sharing breakfast with her, talking about anything and everything. She makes it all feel so easy, so...normal.

I haven't put on the ring she gave me yet. It's not that I didn't appreciate the gesture—I did. Hell, it was the first time anyone had ever given me something so thoughtful without any strings attached. I'm still trying to wrap my head around the fact that she's not like everyone else in my world. She's not after my family's money or angling for power. But the ring...I don't know. It feels like it means more than I'm ready to admit right now. So, it's sitting in my pocket, waiting as I figure out what exactly I want it to represent.

I feel good, though. Better than I thought I would. Arya's smile and energy are infectious, and it's like the stress of the missing money and my father's power games fade into the background when she's around.

"I could get used to this," I say, half-joking, as I sip my coffee. The mood's light, but the truth behind my words lingers.

She glances up at me with her usual bright-eyed curiosity.

"Used to what?" she asks with a small grin.

"Breakfast with you," I admit, not bothering to hide the truth from her. "This—traveling, sharing meals, talking. You make everything feel less…complicated."

She laughs. "I'm glad to be of service."

I take a breath, thinking of something that's been on my mind for a while now—the other thing I promised her. I hate to break out of this happy bubble we're in, but…

"Actually, I've been thinking," I say, setting my coffee down and leaning in slightly. "About your brother. The robbery."

Her face changes almost immediately, a shadow crossing her expression and dimming the brightness in her eyes. Her shoulders visibly tense and she puts her half-eaten piece of toast back on her plate.

"I'm still serious about helping you. I want to know more. The details. How it all went down. From your perspective, I mean. I've heard my family's version."

Arya looks down at her plate. She takes a moment before she speaks, her voice soft.

"It's still hard to talk about. Lou didn't do it. I know that in my bones. He was in the wrong place at the wrong time. Your… your father pinned it all on him, and once they had him, they didn't care about finding anyone else. The stolen items weren't even in his possession."

My jaw clenches. That last detail sticks out to me. If Lou didn't even have the missing jewels, how could they pin anything on him?

"He was framed," I say, more sure of it now than before. "My father's behind it, I'm convinced."

Arya looks at me, a flicker of hope in her eyes, but it's dampened with hesitation.

"But how did your dad get away with it?" she murmurs. "How do we prove Lou's innocent?"

I rub my chin, thinking it over. "We'll need to challenge the conviction. I have some contacts—people who know how to navigate cases like this. I can make some calls, see if we can dig into the evidence that was used against your brother."

She gives me a small, grateful smile, but I can see the sadness lingering in her eyes. This isn't something that'll be fixed overnight, and we both know it. I reach across the table, covering her hand with mine.

"We'll figure it out, Arya. I promise."

She squeezes my hand but doesn't say anything. Her head is dropped and her shoulders slumped. I hate seeing her like this…brought low and despondent.

Wanting to break the tension, I glance around the plane.

"You know," I say, my tone lighter now, "this plane is pretty damn fancy. It'd make a hell of a backdrop for a music video."

Arya blinks, then lets out a surprised laugh. "What?"

"I'm serious," I grin, leaning back in my chair. "Why not shoot a quick video while we're up here? I'll film it for you. We've got your phone, some time to kill, and a pretty cool setting. What do you think?"

She gazes at me without answering, her brow furrowed.. "You'd really do that for me?"

"Of course," I tell her. "What's a doting husband for if not to film his bombshell wife's music videos?"

I watch her take a deep breath and I can see she's doing her best to push away her worries about Lou as she forces a smile and nods.

"Okay, I want to play you something I've been working on. It's a piece I've been composing since…well, since we've been together. It's not done, but we could make a teaser for it to build up some hype."

The way she says that—*since we've been together*—hits me in a way I wasn't expecting. It fills me with warmth and a sense of possession as I gaze at her.

"Play it for me."

Arya grabs her violin and gets ready, moving to stand in the middle of the cabin. I take out her phone and prepare to record the video.

"And, action," I say dramatically.

She grins and lifts her bow to her violin. The moment she starts playing, the entire plane feels like it shifts. The music she creates brimming emotion, so rich and layered. There's something romantic about the song. It makes me imagine kissing her in the moonlight, sweeping her off her feet and making love to her under the stars. My heart begins to beat harder and harder, and I lose my breath as she continues to play.

When she finishes, there's a quiet moment between us, filled only by the soft hum of the plane. She nods to the phone that I'm still holding out like an idiot, the video still running while I stare at her.

I scramble to shut it off. "That was incredible."

She blushes. "You think so?"

"It practically gave me chills—people will be crazy for it," I say. "Now, let's get a few different shots and really make this video pop."

We spend the next hour choreographing quick shots, working around the space of the plane, her playing while I continue to film. It's all so natural, so fun, and for the first time in days, I feel like I'm not just running from one problem to the next. Arya's music saturates the space, and her joy infects me.

As I'm holding Arya's phone, adjusting the angle to catch the perfect light streaming in through the plane's windows, a buzz shakes the screen. I ignore it at first, focusing on the video.

Another buzz.

Finally, when the third buzz comes through, I check the screen in irritation.

It's a text from an unknown number.

> I know what you're doing. You think you're
> going to scam your way into my family's
> money? You won't succeed. Walk away now,
> or you'll regret it.

My stomach churns as I realize I know this number. It's my dad's. His condescending tone practically oozes through the screen. The bastard must've found Arya's number and decided to bypass me completely, going straight for her.

The phone buzzes again.

> You're not the first gold digger to try this.
> Leave my son alone or I will destroy you.

Did he *threaten* her? My pulse spikes, anger curling hot and sharp in my chest. How *dare* he? How dare he insert himself into something that has nothing to do with him. Arya isn't a gold digger, and the fact that my father keeps hammering that idea is pissing me off.

Thankfully, Arya has no idea what's happening. She's still playing, smiling, caught in the moment, and I'll be damned if I let him ruin this for her.

Without thinking twice, I swipe the messages away, deleting them, my jaw clenched. Then, I block the number entirely, cutting off any chance of more messages coming through. If he wants to pull this kind of crap, he'll have to do it directly with me. I'm not letting him drag Arya into his games, not when she has enough on her plate already.

The satisfaction of blocking him simmers in my chest, but it doesn't erase the growing urge I feel to confront him. To tell him to his face that I'm not his puppet, and Arya doesn't deserve to be caught up in his need to control his whole family.

I take a breath, forcing myself to focus on the video.

"Almost done," I tell her, trying to keep my tone steady.

Arya flashes me a wide grin, oblivious to the storm raging inside me. "Take your time. I'm having fun."

Just like that, I feel the anger fade a little. She's so easygoing, so full of light—it's hard to stay angry when she's smiling like that.

———

A few hours later, we land in New York. Arya suggests getting a hotel, something central where we can stay for a few days while she prepares for her Carnegie audition—but I have a better idea. One that's sure to get under my father's skin in a way that no text message could.

"No hotel," I say casually as we walk through the airport, bags in hand. "We'll stay at the family brownstone."

Arya blinks in surprise. "Wait, the family brownstone? Won't your dad—"

I smirk, cutting her off. "My brother Andrew's out of town. He runs the family's logistics company up here, and he's on a business trip. It'll just be us."

She looks at me for a beat, and then shrugs. "Alright, I'm in. But are you sure it's a good idea?"

"It'll be fine. Besides, what's the point of having a fancy home in New York if we can't use it?"

In truth, there's more to it than that. Staying at the brownstone feels like a way to reclaim a little bit of control—control that my father keeps trying to strip away from me. If he finds out we're staying there? Even better. It'll drive him nuts. After the texts he sent Arya, I'm more than happy to push his buttons.

It's not my father I'm thinking about as I usher her into the car waiting for us. Bringing Arya to my family's home feels oddly significant. Permanent in a way that excites me more than I'll admit. Suddenly, we feel more like an "us" than two people hooking up on a tour and even though it's foolish, I want to hold onto that feeling.

That confrontation with my father, especially now that he's threatened her? It's coming.

THE NEXT MORNING, I blink open my eyes, and it takes me a moment to remember where I am; the now familiar sunlit bedroom with gauzy white curtains framing the tall windows, lightly colored furniture, paintings hanging on the walls, and a king-size bed that I'm buried in.

My lips curl into a delighted smile as I roll over, expecting to find him in bed next to me.

He's not there.

"Ethan?" I call out, but there's no answer. I push down my disappointment at his absence. He probably just ran out for something and will be right back. Nothing to worry about.

I climb out of bed and get dressed, then make my way out of the bedroom. My mind shifts from thoughts of Ethan to my audition this afternoon. I can hardly believe it's finally happening, and the more I think about it, the more my heart races and anxiety bubbles up in my stomach. By the time I reach the kitchen with its large island and state-of-the art appliances, I'm so jittery, I know eating is a terrible idea. The last thing I want is to puke up a yogurt parfait at my audition.

I settle on some orange juice. Drinking a bit helps settle my stomach some, but there's really only one thing that will help me calm down: playing. Well, two things. I could really use Ethan's company right now. His support and confidence in me is so steady, so comforting, he makes me feel like I can conquer the world.

But it's just me and my OJ right now, so I grab my violin case, which is sitting on the island, and open it. Pulling out the instrument, I settle it under my chin and pick up my bow. Without thinking twice, I play the piece I've been composing since I started this wild trip.

The one I played on the plane while Ethan videoed me. The one I've actually been writing for him, though I haven't told him that yet. My music is such an intimate, vital part of me, that creating a song for someone is…well…it's actually something I've never done before. I've written songs about people, like Lou, but as a way of processing my feelings and not as something to present to them as some sort of gift.

This song…this song is different. When it's done, I want everyone who hears it to know who it's been written for. I don't want to hide the meaning behind the music, just as I don't want to hide my feelings for Ethan.

As I play, I dance around the kitchen and let the music sweep me away, into the living room. I close my eyes, getting lost in the harmony. My anxiety eases slightly, replaced by the soothing familiarity of the strings beneath my fingers. I'm so absorbed in the music that I almost don't hear the sound of a key turning in the lock of the front door.

My eyes snap open, and I pause my playing as a smile spreads across my face. Ethan must be back from whatever errand he was running. Perfect timing. I start playing again, anticipating the look on his face when I tell him the song is for him.

But when the door swings open, it's not Ethan who steps inside.

It's Jared Cavenwell.

My hands freeze on the strings, the last note hanging awkwardly in the air before dissipating into stunned silence. I stare at him in shock as he closes the door behind him with a deliberate click, his eyes never leaving mine.

"It appears you've made yourself right at home," he snarls, venom dripping from each word.

Swallowing, I fight to maintain my composure as my rage burns through my shock at seeing him. "What are you doing here? Ethan wasn't expecting anyone to be here but us."

He nods, crossing the room to stand directly in front of me.

"My son seems to have forgotten that this is my property, and I can show up whenever I damn well please."

"We both know you didn't just pop up to New York to say hi," I snap, my fury spiking when he mentions Ethan's name.

He tilts his head and regards me before replying, "You think you're smart, playing your little game with Ethan, don't you?"

I furrow my brow and shake my head. "I have no idea what you're talking about."

"I know what you're doing. Using him to get what you want. You're the first gold-digger to ever go after Ethan, so he's too naive to see your true intentions. I am not."

The accusation hits like a slap, and my chest tightens with a mix of shock and anger.

"I'm not using Ethan," I say firmly, my voice steady even though my hands start to shake. "I care about him."

Jared scoffs, crossing his arms. "Yeah, that's what they all say. 'I care about him.' But you're not fooling me. You're just like the others—chasing the family fortune."

I take a step back, my pulse racing, but I stop myself. I don't want this man to think he can intimidate me.

"You don't know anything about me," I say in a cold voice. I can hardly believe this bastard's hypocrisy. Accusing me of using Ethan when he used Lou like a pawn and he's now trying to manipulate Ethan to force him into being who he wants him to be. It's infuriating.

"Oh, I know plenty," he sneers. "I figured out who you really are. Didn't you think I'd dig into my new daughter-in-law's past to find out her real motivations for marrying my son? I know all about your junky mother and scumbag stepbrother. No wonder you're looking to cash in on Ethan. Crime runs in your blood."

I grit my teeth and curl my hands into fists. This asshole is unbelievable. He's a monster and has the gall to look down his nose on me and my family.

"Don't talk about my family like that," I hiss.

Jared's eyes narrow. "Your brother's a thief. He stole from my family, and now you think you can worm your way into our lives and do the same? It's pathetic."

"My brother didn't steal anything from you!" I shout, stepping toward him, anger pulsing through me. "You lied to the police, and you know it. You accused him and ruined both our lives! I'll never stop trying to clear his name and prove what a monster you really are."

Jared's eyes darken even more, and the tension between us is so thick it feels like the air itself could crack like glass.

"You'll never prove anything," he says coldly. "And if you know what's good for you, you'll leave Ethan before you drag him down with your mess."

I grit my teeth, fury boiling beneath my skin.

"I love Ethan," I say, my voice shaking with emotion. As soon as the words are past my lips, I freeze, shocked. Do I love Ethan?

Yes...yes I do. I've been so focused on my tour and preparing for my audition that I didn't realize I was falling for him, but it's so clear now. Ethan is the first person since Lou to support me unconditionally. He doesn't look down on me, doesn't think I'm foolish for chasing my dreams. When I'm with

Ethan, I feel safe, cared for, and comfortable enough to let my guard down. I gave my heart to him, and it happened so naturally that I didn't notice.

"I'm not going anywhere," I continue, my voice thick with determination. "You can insult me, insult my family, but you don't get to decide what happens between me and him."

"Love?" Jared lets out a bark of cold, cruel laughter. "Maybe you can fool Ethan with that bullshit, but you can't fool me, you greedy bitch."

"As if you know anything about love," I snarl. "You use people and don't give a shit who you plow over to get what you want. I don't think you even know what love is."

"I'll make it simple," he says, ignoring my accusation. His expression shifts from anger to something even more dangerous —a calculated, manipulative calm. "How much will it take? What's your price to leave Ethan? I'll write you a check right now, and you can walk away with no problems."

I stare at him, my mind reeling. Is he serious? Does he really think I'd take his money? I straighten my back, feeling the fire return to my voice.

"I'm not interested in your money."

He tilts his head, considering me, and a cold smile curls on his lips. "Fine. Maybe money isn't what you're after." His voice drops lower, colder. "But what if I told you I could make your brother's life in prison a lot worse? Or maybe…" He steps even closer, his eyes dark with something that sends a chill down my spine. "Maybe something could happen to *you*. Or to Ethan."

The air freezes around me. My throat tightens, my hands shaking as fear grips me. He's not bluffing. I can see it in his eyes—he's capable of it. Of hurting me, hurting my brother. Hurting *Ethan*. His own son. Maybe not physically, but he'll do whatever he thinks will break Ethan's spirit so that he's left an empty shell that Jared can control like a puppet. That'd be a fate almost worse than death for Ethan. My chest tightens, and for a second, I can't breathe.

"You wouldn't—" I start, but the tremor in my voice betrays me. I know, deep down, that Jared is the kind of man who would follow through on his threats. He's not bluffing. I can feel it in the way he's looking at me, like a predator toying with his prey.

"You know I can," he says softly, his voice dripping with malice. "Anyone who gets in the way of me and my ambitions is expendable...even Ethan. So here's the deal. You leave Ethan. Walk away, right now. You never look back, and maybe, just maybe, nothing happens to your brother. Or to you. Or to Ethan."

The weight of his words crashes over me, and for the first time since he walked in, I feel completely powerless. The thought of anything happening to Ethan...or my brother...I can't. I *won't* let that happen.

I swallow hard, my voice barely above a whisper. "Fine. I'll leave Ethan. But I don't want your money."

Jared smirks, the triumph in his eyes making me feel sick. "Smart girl."

My heart shatters into pieces as I turn away from him, my hands shaking as I walk to the bedroom. I can barely think as I grab my violin cases, throwing my belongings together in a daze. This isn't how the day was supposed to go. I'm supposed to go kill it at my audition and come back here to Ethan, thrilled by my success. He'd take me in his arms and we'd make love all night, celebrating and then losing ourselves in each other.

That's not going to happen now. I'm not coming back to Ethan, and that is such a devastating thought, I think I might be sick.

I walk into the kitchen and pause next to the island. Looking down at the ring on my finger, I think about what it has come to mean to me. It was once just a reminder of every awful thing that's happened to me and my brother—of how Jared broke us apart and ruined our lives for his own selfish gain. I hated this ring when I realized it was part of Jared's schemes, but now...

now it reminds me of everything that I've been through to get to Ethan.

When I look at the ring, I still think of Lou and how badly I miss him, but now I also think of Ethan. I think of our wedding, when he pulled me into a supply closet to calm my nerves and reassure me that our plan would work. When he stood up to that bar owner who was trying to rip me off. When he kept a hair tie around his wrist for me because he knew I'd misplace mine. All the times we were intimate, and he touched me like he adored me and kissed me like he couldn't get enough of me.

I have to fight back tears as I slide the ring off and set it on the countertop.

Reaching the living room again, I glare up at Jared, my voice steady despite the tears threatening to spill over. "I'll leave Ethan alone, but I'm not done with you. I'll keep digging. I'll find a way to prove my brother's innocence, no matter how long it takes."

Jared laughs, a harsh, bitter sound that makes my skin crawl. "Good luck with that."

I don't respond. I can't. The only thing I can do now is leave. As I step outside the brownstone, I catch a glimpse of Ethan. He's walking up the sidewalk, a bouquet of flowers in hand, a small smile on his face like he's excited to see me. My chest tightens, and I feel the tears brimming in my eyes. I can't face him. If I look at him…if I talk to him…I won't be able to walk away from him. I'll tell him how I feel about him, and I can't risk doing that.

I hurry in the opposite direction before Ethan can see me and quickly flag down a taxi, sliding into the back seat as the tears finally spill over. I tell the driver to take me to Carnegie Hall, even though I can barely think past the heartbreak and fear clouding my mind.

I don't know what I'm going to do after the audition. I don't know where I'll go, but I can't stay with Ethan. Not if it means putting him in danger. The thought of leaving him, of never seeing him again, breaks something inside me.

As the city streets blur outside the taxi window, I wipe at my tears, trying to pull myself together. I have to focus on the audition. One step at a time.

But deep down, I know I'll never be the same without him.

Chapter Twenty-Two

ETHAN

I'M CONFUSED as I watch Arya disappear down the street, sliding into a taxi with her violin cases and suitcase. She didn't even look back. I'd come back with flowers, ready to surprise her, and instead, I see her leaving with all her things.

Is she leaving me? No...no, that's not it. She wouldn't do that, not after the nights we just spent together. *Why does she have all of her things, then?* The idea of her slipping away like that gnaws at me. It's unsettling in a way I can't quite shake.

With a sigh, I make my way up the steps to the brownstone, trying to push the uneasy feeling aside. Maybe she just needed some space. Maybe she's nervous about her audition. I open the door, stepping inside, the familiar scent of the place grounding me a little as I set the flowers on the kitchen counter.

Then I see it.

The ring. Sitting there, gleaming on the kitchen island like it's mocking me. Shock slams through me, cold and sharp. What the hell is this doing here? My mind scrambles, searching for an explanation. She wouldn't just leave, not like this. If I did something wrong, she wouldn't hesitate to let me know about it. She'd rip into me and make sure I knew exactly why she was done with me.

Yet, there's the ring and Arya just took off in a cab without a backward glance.

A rush of panic floods my system. I grab the ring, holding it in my palm, the weight of it feeling suddenly unbearable. She's gone. She *left*. And she didn't even say a word. The flowers sit forgotten on the counter as my heart hammers in my chest. How could she just leave without saying anything?

I'm about to turn around and rush out to chase after her when I hear a noise coming from the study. I freeze, the hairs on the back of my neck standing up. Someone's in the house. No one is supposed to be here except Arya and me.

My jaw clenches as I walk toward the study, the ring still gripped tightly in my hand. When I push the door open, my blood instantly boils with fury.

My father stands by the open wall safe, casually pulling a box from it. He's calm, too calm, like he doesn't have a care in the world. The sight of him makes my stomach churn with rage.

"What the hell are you doing here?" I demand, stepping into the room, my voice rough with anger. "Why did Arya leave? What did you say to her?"

Dad doesn't even flinch. He turns to face me, a slow, smug smile creeping onto his face as he closes the safe behind him.

"Ah, Ethan. I was wondering when you'd show up." He says it like he's been expecting this moment, like he's already won.

"I asked you a question," I snap, stepping closer. "What did you do?"

His smile widens, and I can feel the sick satisfaction radiating off him.

"Arya?" he says, his voice dripping with false sympathy. "She's gone, Ethan. Took the money and ran. Exactly like I said she would."

My heart stutters. "What are you talking about?"

He leans against the desk, looking too relaxed, too in control. "I offered her a check. A substantial one, and she took it.

Walked out of here without a second thought. A gold digger, just like I told you from the beginning."

No. That can't be true. Arya wouldn't—she wouldn't take money from him. Not after everything we've been through. My chest tightens, panic and fury clashing inside me.

"You're lying," I spit, shaking my head. "You're lying. She wouldn't do that."

Dad's expression darkens, his smile fading into something colder. "It's over, Ethan. She's gone. And now you have a choice." He straightens, stepping forward, his voice low and menacing. "You can come back to the family. Work for me—either in the business or in the political office. Try to rebuild your name, and all will be forgiven. Or…"

He lets the silence stretch, the threat sinking in before finishing.

"Or I drain your accounts. Everything you have left. You'll be out of options. Out of money. You can decide if being stubborn is really worth it."

My father's words—*drain your account*—set off a deep, seething rage inside me. It starts as a low hum, building with each breath, until it's pounding in my ears. Drain my account? Like he drained the trust fund he was supposed to be stewarding for *me*?

"You already drained my accounts!" I shout. "I know you stole the money out of my trust. The money in my personal account is nothing compared to what you've already taken, and I swear to God I'm not going to let you get away with it."

Dad rolls his eyes at me. "What exactly are you going to do? If you were more like your brothers or sister, I might be concerned, but I don't expect much from you when you're on your own." He starts to move toward the door.

I turn, blocking his path, my eyes locking onto his.

"What's in the safe, Dad?" My voice is cold, but underneath it is a dangerous edge, a fury that's been simmering for far too long. "What are you hiding in there?"

"That's none of your business," he hisses, trying to get around me again, but I don't let him slip by.

"Arya isn't a gold digger. I know she isn't. You know how I know that?" I step closer, forcing him to meet my gaze. "Because she was prepared to have my back even if I ran out of money. Even if I had *nothing*."

The smirk falters, and I press on. "Now, tell me what's in the safe. Or I'll find out for myself."

He stares at me, his jaw tightening, but I'm done playing his games. I don't wait for his permission—I grab the box he pulled from the wall safe. He tries to resist, but I'm stronger and yank it from his grasp. It's heavy in my hands.

Opening the lid, I find that inside, nestled in dark velvet, are glittering pieces of jewelry. Expensive ones. Familiar ones. I stare at them, my breath catching in my throat as the realization hits me. These are the stolen jewels from *years ago*, the ones that got Arya's brother falsely accused, the ones that destroyed her family's life.

My eyes flicker to Dad, who's watching me with a calculating look. For the first time, I see him for exactly who he is—someone willing to destroy anyone to keep his world intact. He doesn't even flinch as the truth dawns on me.

"You took these," I say, my voice low and deadly. "You stole these for the insurance money."

He crosses his arms, his expression cold and unapologetic. "I did what had to be done. I made some investments that went poorly, and I couldn't let our family lose face. The board of directors would have doubted my ability to run the businesses within the conglomerate, and my constituents wouldn't have been so keen to reelect me if they found out about our financial drop. We needed the money, and the insurance for the jewels paid out handsomely."

My stomach turns. All this was because my dad fucked up the family's finances and refused to own up to his mistakes. He's more concerned about maintaining appearances than about ruining the life of a total stranger who never did anything to our family. This whole time, Arya's brother had been innocent, and now I'm holding the proof in my hands.

Jared steps forward, his voice lowering into that persuasive tone he always uses when he's trying to manipulate me. "We can make this go away, Ethan. We'll sell the jewels, and no one will ever know about any of this. I'll admit, I was worried when you found the ring in Texas, so I moved the rest of the jewels here. Honestly, I should have sold them years ago, but I knew the cops would be keeping an eye for them. Now, though, no one will notice. We'll wash our hands of this whole mess and you'll come home. All will be forgiven."

The offer hangs in the air. The money. My future. Everything I thought I wanted.

But when I look down at the jewels, all I can think about is Arya. Her face, her voice, her unwavering belief in her brother's innocence. I realize the money doesn't matter. None of it matters without her.

I close the box slowly, my decision crystallizing in my mind.

"No," I say, my voice steady. "I'm done."

Jared's eyes narrow, realizing what I'm about to do. "Ethan—"

I cut him off, pulling out my phone. "I'm calling the police."

The color drains from his face. "Ethan, think about what you're doing. If you go through with this, you'll be throwing away your entire future. Your family's entire future. Everything."

"I don't care," I say, my voice filled with a clarity I haven't felt in years. "This ends now."

As I make the call, Dad dodges for the door, but I block him. He's tall, but lean, and I've got more muscle. We both know I can take him to the floor if need be.

Within minutes, the police arrive. Dad tries to argue, and when that doesn't work, to make deals, which only earns him new charges for attempting to bribe the cops. I hand over the jewels and explain everything to the cops. The officers handcuff him, leading him out of the brownstone while I watch, a strange sense of calm settling over me. I should feel more triumphant, but all I can think about is Arya.

As Dad is escorted out the door, he looks at me, his lips curling into a cruel smile.

"I was right about one thing," he gloats, his voice dripping with satisfaction. "Arya's gone. Left you as soon as she got the money she was after. Just like I said she would."

My heart sinks, the weight of his words hitting me like a blow. Did she really take his money? For one second I believe him. *It would really help her…*

No. Arya wouldn't do that to me. She's not that kind of person. She's kind, sweet, and knows what it's like to be screwed over, so she would never dream of hurting someone in a similar way. She's too good, despite how messed up her life has been. She came into my life, shining like the sun, and chased away the shadows narrowing my vision. She made me want more out of life. Before her, I only cared about the trust and breaking free of my father. Now, I care about her.

No…it's more than that.

I love her.

I'm in love with Arya.

I swallow hard, fighting the rising panic that comes with that realization and knowing that she's gone. I don't know why she left, what he said to her, but I need to find her and fix this. *Now.*

I don't wait another second. The moment Dad is out the door, I grab my jacket, my mind racing. There's only one place she could be—*Carnegie Hall.* Her audition.

I burst out of the brownstone, running through the city streets as the sun dips below the horizon, casting everything in a fiery glow. My heart pounds in time with my footsteps, my mind fixed on one thing—*finding Arya.*

I can't lose her. Not now. Not ever.

Chapter Twenty-Three

ARYA

I SIT in the dimly lit waiting area, my hands gripping the violin case in my lap so tightly that my knuckles are white. My heart pounds in my chest, every beat like a hammer against my ribs. I try to focus on breathing, on calming down, but I can't stop the tears that keep welling up in my eyes. I blink them back quickly, not wanting anyone to see.

This is supposed to be my moment—my chance to play for the hiring committee at Carnegie Hall, but all I can think about is Ethan. The thought of never seeing him again, never hearing his voice or seeing his smile, makes my chest ache in a way I can't describe. It's like something's been torn out of me, and I don't know how to fill the space.

When I gave Ethan that ring, there was something in his expression that made me believe what was happening between us was real. That maybe he wanted the marriage to continue, to make it permanent, even after my audition and the terms of our deal were technically met. I'd started thinking of a future together, but that was foolish of me. His father will always be a threat, and if we're together, Ethan and I will never be able to live in peace.

My mind keeps spinning in circles, and for the first time in years, my patented technique of changing my attitude is failing me. Everything just feels wrong. Not having Ethan here to cheer me on is gutting me.

Tish, who showed up at the last minute to support me, sits next to me, but even she seems skeptical. She keeps glancing at me like she's waiting for me to pull it together, to be the Arya she knows—the one who always finds a way to make it through. But I can't. Not today.

"How are you holding up?" Tish asks, her voice soft, though there's an edge of doubt in it.

I shake my head, trying to force a smile. "I'm fine. I have to be amazing, right? There's no other option." My voice cracks on the last word, betraying how unsteady I really am.

Tish raises an eyebrow. "You sure about that? You don't... seem like yourself."

I laugh bitterly, wiping at my eyes. "I'm not, Tish. I'm really not. I was so close to everything I wanted. And now? I don't even know where I'm going to sleep tonight."

She gives me a sympathetic look, but before she can reply, my name is called, and the sound of it sends a jolt of panic through me. This is it. The moment I've been waiting for. But as I stand, my legs feel like they might give out under me. I paste a dazzling smile on my face, trying to convince myself that I can do this, that I can still make them hire me on the spot.

As I walk onto the stage, the lights are blinding, the room too quiet. The committee members sit in a line, their faces impossible to make out because of the lights, waiting for me to start. I take a deep breath, positioning my violin under my chin. My fingers tremble slightly as I raise the bow.

The first note comes out shaky, thin. I cringe, but keep playing, forcing myself to push through it. No matter how hard I try, I can't seem to find the rhythm. The music that usually flows from me so naturally feels stilted and wrong. My heart isn't in it. It's broken, and I don't know how to put it back together right now.

I can see the committee members turning to look at each other, and my stomach twists even though I can't see their expressions. I try to smile again, to keep up the act, but it's no use. The notes falter, my bow slipping awkwardly on the strings. I can feel the failure building with every second, like a weight pressing down on me.

When the piece ends, the silence that follows is deafening. I lower my violin, staring out at the committee, but their faces are unreadable. My smile fades, the reality sinking in.

I've failed.

"Thank you," one of the committee members says in a voice layered with exasperation. "You can go."

I force myself to walk off the stage, my heart heavy, my mind numb. Tish doesn't say anything as I return to the waiting area, and I can't bear to look at her. I already know what she's thinking.

I've fucked this up beyond repair.

I barely register Tish's voice beside me as she talks about getting us a cheap hotel, just something to tide us over until I figure out what to do next. The words pass through me like a breeze, not quite landing, not quite making sense. My mind is still in that audition room, on the stage where I failed. Where everything I've worked for slipped through my fingers.

Tish guides me out a side door, away from the crowd of other applicants, their hopeful chatter fading into the background. I step out onto the curb, the sticky New York air hitting my skin, but it does nothing to shake the numbness clinging to me.

It's over.

Everything I've fought for—my music, my dreams, even Ethan—gone. I don't know what to do, where to go. How did it all fall apart so fast?

Tish hails a cab, her voice rising over the city noise, but I barely hear her. My thoughts are scattered, lost in the chaos of it all. I just stand there, staring at nothing, wondering what's supposed to come next when everything I've built has crumbled in an instant.

Then, out of nowhere, I hear the screech of tires.

Before I can react, something slams into me. The impact knocks me off my feet, and I don't even realize what's happened until I feel the cold pavement beneath me. My head hits the ground, a sharp pain shooting through my skull.

The last thing I remember is the sound of Tish screaming my name.

Then, everything goes dark.

Chapter Twenty-Four

ARYA

I WAKE up to a soft beeping sound. My body feels heavy and groggy. The air smells sterile, like antiseptic, and the sheets beneath my fingers are too crisp. Too stiff. My head throbs, and I blink slowly, trying to make sense of where I am.

A hospital.

I'm in a hospital bed.

Panic flares in my chest as my foggy mind struggles to catch up. I try to sit up, but my limbs feel like they're weighed down, sluggish from whatever painkillers are coursing through my system. The events of the day slowly start to piece themselves together—Jared, the audition, the screeching tires. The impact. My violin.

I glance to the side and freeze. Ethan's here. He's slumped in a chair next to the bed, his head resting on his folded arms, and he's fast asleep. How is he here? How did he find out about the accident? Did Tish tell him? Just like that, my heart starts racing for a completely different reason.

Danger. He's in danger.

My breathing picks up, and I look around for a way out, something, anything to get me out of here before it's too late. I need to leave. I can't stay—not with Ethan here. He's been through so much already, and I can't stand the thought of his father continuing to hurt him because he's with me.

I shift, trying to slide out of the bed as quietly as possible, even if it means sneaking out in this flimsy hospital gown. I just need to get away. As I begin to move, however, Ethan stirs. His eyes blink open, disoriented for a moment, until they lock onto me.

"Arya!" His voice is thick with relief, and before I can say anything, he's on his feet and pulling me into his arms. The sudden movement makes my head spin, but the feel of his arms around me, his warmth and strength, stops me from fighting. He holds me so tightly, like he thought he'd never see me again.

Then his lips are on mine in a kiss that takes my breath away. It's desperate, raw, and full of emotion that overwhelms me. He pulls back slightly, resting his forehead against mine, and I can feel him trembling.

"I thought—" His voice cracks. "I thought I lost you."

The panic inside me ebbs as his words sink in and the sheer relief in his voice washes over me. I look up at him, confusion mixing with everything else.

"Ethan…what are you doing here? You…you're in danger."

His brow furrows, and he shakes his head. "No, Arya. You're safe now. We're safe."

My heart stutters, the fear still gnawing at me. "But your father—"

"He can't hurt us," Ethan interrupts, his voice firm but soft, like he's trying to calm me. "Dad's been arrested."

"What?" I blink, struggling to comprehend what he's saying. "Arrested? For what?"

Ethan steps back slightly, his hands still holding mine as he takes a deep breath. "For everything. The robbery, the lies about your brother. The jewelry, the whole setup—he did it all for the insurance money. He can deny it all he wants, but I caught him pulling the jewels out of the safe in the brownstone. That's more than enough to charge him."

I stare at him, my mind reeling.

My heart races, trying to keep up with everything. Jared's gone, and the danger I thought Ethan was in…it's over?

Then it hits me: Lou.

"Does…does that mean…?" I can hardly say the words, my voice is so choked with emotion.

Ethan smiles and brushes his fingers down my cheek. He knows exactly what I'm asking. "Yeah, we're going to clear Lou's name, sweetheart. You're going to get your brother back."

A sob of joy breaks from me and I wrap my arms around Ethan, hugging him tight. He holds me as I cry against his shoulder, the relief and happiness knowing that I'm finally going to free my brother overwhelming me.

After a few minutes, I manage to bring myself under control and lean back to look up at him.

"The trust fund?" I ask, my voice barely above a whisper.

Ethan nods, his expression softening. "It's all coming back to me. Every penny. Jesse talked to Gerald, who's been holding the money in a private account. He didn't realize my father had stolen it from me…at least, that's what he says. He's making sure it's all returned, though. My father's out of the picture, and I'm free from him—finally."

The rush of everything hits me all at once, and I feel a little dizzy again. Ethan, his father, the confession…it's a lot to process. Then something catches my eye that distracts me. I blink and realize that Ethan's wearing his ring. The one I bought for him in Las Vegas.

A quiet laugh escapes me, even though I'm still trying to make sense of everything.

"You're wearing it?" I murmur, looking up at him with a wide smile.

Ethan gives me a sheepish grin, rubbing the back of his neck like he's embarrassed. "Yeah…and I have something for you."

Before I can respond, he reaches into his pocket and pulls something out—a small box. My heart skips a beat as he opens it, revealing a gorgeous ring with a princess cut diamond set in a white gold band.

"Here," he says, his voice soft but sure. "I wanted to get you a new one. The old one has too many bad memories attached to it, and I want us to have a fresh start. For real this time. No contracts. No deals. Just me and you. When it came down to it, Arya, I realized I was more afraid of losing you than I ever was of losing the money. I want to marry you, Arya, for real this time. I want to be your husband, and I want you to be my wife."

My breath catches, and I feel a wave of emotion wash over me—relief, happiness, and excitement all rolled into one. I stare at the ring, and then back at him. This man, who I thought I had to leave behind, who I thought I could never have because of everything pulling us apart.

Yet, he's here, and I'm still here. Somehow, despite everything, he's offering me this. Not just the ring—but him. Us.

"I..." I start, my voice shaking a little. "I don't know what to say."

Ethan's smile softens, his eyes searching mine. "Say yes. Just take it. Take me. I love you, Arya. I want to spend the rest of my life with you."

The tears I'd been holding back spill over, but this time, they're not from fear or heartbreak. They're from the overwhelming relief of being offered something real. Something that isn't tied to money or expectations.

I nod, my fingers trembling as I take the ring from his hand.

"Yes," I whisper, slipping it onto my finger. "I'll take you. All of it. I love you too."

His eyes widen and his lips part as he gazes at me, seemingly stunned, then he grins like a fool. The moment feels surreal, almost like I'm still half-dreaming.

The next second, Ethan grins, pulling me into his arms again, and I let out a soft laugh, wiping the tears from my cheeks. But then, the reality of everything else catches up with me, and my smile falters.

"I have to tell you something," I murmur, leaning my forehead against his chest. "I failed the audition. I completely bombed it. I have no idea what I'm going to do next. I don't know where to go from here."

Ethan pulls back slightly, looking down at me with a teasing glint in his eyes. "No idea, huh?"

I shake my head, feeling that old familiar uncertainty rising again. "Yeah. I was so sure of everything, but now? I just feel… lost."

He chuckles, tucking a strand of hair behind my ear. "Well, lucky for you, I might have a few ideas."

I raise an eyebrow, curiosity piqued despite myself. "Oh, really?"

"Yeah," he says, his grin widening. "How about this…we'll take a little time to figure it out together. No pressure. No rush. Just you and me, and whatever comes next."

My shoulders relax, the weight of everything starting to lift. "I think I like the sound of that."

Ethan leans down, pressing a soft kiss to my forehead.

"Good," he whispers against my skin. "Because I'm not letting you go again, Arya. We're in this together."

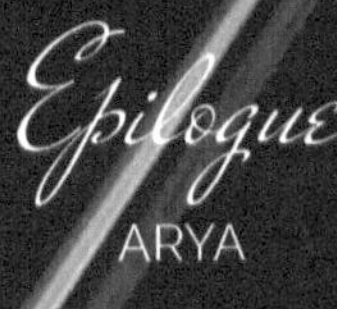

Epilogue
ARYA

IT'S strange how time warps—how the weeks leading up to this moment have felt like both an eternity and the blink of an eye. I've been waiting for this day for what feels like forever, but now that it's here, my nerves are a mess. I'm standing outside the prison gates, watching the doors where my brother, Lou, is about to walk out.

Ethan was able to hire a lawyer and get Lou's case over-turned. Ironically, he's been being held in New Jersey, so we're able to meet him as he's released. My hands are fidgeting at my sides, my heart racing in my chest. Ethan is standing a little behind me, giving me space but close enough to let me know he's here. His presence calms me, but it doesn't take away the overwhelming anticipation coursing through me.

Then, finally, I see him.

Lou steps out, looking different from the last time I saw him. Thinner. Older. With more tattoos. But his eyes—they're the same. The same sharp, bright eyes I've always known. And when his gaze lands on me, I can see the flicker of disbelief, like he can't quite believe he's really out, or that I'm really here, waiting for him.

For a moment, neither of us moves. We just stare at each other, as if neither of us knows what to do.

Then, we're rushing toward each other. I throw my arms around him, squeezing him so tight it's like I'm afraid he'll slip away if I let go.

"Lou," I whisper, my voice thick with emotion, my face buried in his shoulder. "You're okay."

He holds me just as tightly, his grip strong, almost desperate.

"Arya," he breathes, his voice rough, like he hasn't spoken much in a while. "God, I missed you."

I pull back just enough to look at him, my hands still gripping his arms as if to make sure he's real. "I missed you, too. So much."

He gives me a small, tired smile, his eyes scanning my face like he's trying to memorize every detail.

"You're still the same," he says softly, but there's a sadness in his voice, too. "But I can't say the same for me."

Tears prick at my eyes, but I blink them back. "We'll figure it out, Lou. We'll get through this. You're free now."

"Yeah," he says almost reverently. "Free."

I take his hand, squeezing it tightly. "I'm going to help you, just like I promised. You took care of me growing up, and now it's my turn to take care of you."

He looks at me, his expression softening. "I don't know how to thank you for believing me and fighting for me all these years."

"You don't have to," I say quickly, my voice breaking. "You're my brother. That's what family does."

We just stand there, holding onto each other. The world around us feels far away, like it's just me and Lou after everything we've been through. But I feel Ethan's presence behind me, steady and sure.

I glance over my shoulder at Ethan, who's watching us with a soft smile. He steps forward, nodding at Lou.

"Good to finally meet you," Ethan says. "Arya's been waiting for this day for a long time."

Lou looks between me and Ethan, a flicker of curiosity in his eyes. "So, you're the guy, huh?"

Ethan chuckles, rubbing the back of his neck. "Yeah. I guess so."

Lou's smile widens, but I can see the protective older brother instinct kicking in, even after everything he's been through.

"I'm glad you were there for her," he says, his tone serious. "She needed someone in her corner."

Ethan steps forward, offering his hand. "I'll always be there for her."

Lou shakes his hand and I feel like my heart is going to burst open with joy. I take a deep breath, looking between the two most important men in my life.

"Let's get out of here," I say, feeling a surge of hope I haven't felt in a long time. "It's time to start over."

Lou nods, and together, the three of us walk away from the prison gates, leaving the past behind us.

———

The lights of Carnegie Hall feel like pure magic as I step onto the stage, my violin in hand. My heart pounds, not with nerves, but with excitement. I've always thrived in moments like these —where the world fades away and it's just me, my music, and the audience waiting to be taken on a journey.

I can feel the energy from the crowd humming through the air, and I let it fuel me. Somewhere in the wings, I know Ethan is there, watching me with that look of quiet pride he always has when I'm doing what I love. His belief in me has been a constant, and tonight, I want to show him just how much that means.

I step into the center of the stage, taking a deep breath as the lights dim slightly, focusing all their brilliance on me. The hall is packed, but it's the intimacy of the moment that wraps around me. This is my time.

Gazing out over the crowd, I lean toward the microphone standing in front of me and say, "This song is very special to me. I wrote it for the love of my life, Ethan Cavenwell, and I want to share it with all of you for the first time publicly tonight."

The crowd cheers and with a smooth movement, I lift my bow to the strings and let the first note soar through the room, filling every inch of the space with the rich, warm sound of my violin. The music flows from me, each note cascading into the next, my heart pouring into the melody. I lose myself in it, letting the energy of the crowd push me higher, letting the passion I feel for this moment radiate from every note.

It feels like I'm flying, like this performance is the culmination of every dream I've ever had. I can see the faces in the audience—captivated, listening intently—and I know that this is what I was born to do.

When I finish the final piece, the applause is thunderous, and for a moment, I just stand there, soaking it in, my chest heaving with the thrill of the performance. The lights are blinding, but I can feel the warmth of the crowd, the validation that every late night, every sacrifice, has been worth it.

As I step off the stage, my body still buzzing with adrenaline, I see Ethan standing there, waiting for me just like I knew he would be. Right beside him is Lou, looking prouder than I've ever seen him.

Tears spring to my eyes, and before I can stop myself, I'm running to him, wrapping my arms around him in the tightest hug I can manage.

"I can hardly believe you're really here," I whisper, my voice thick with emotion. "You heard me play."

Lou pulls back slightly, looking down at me with a warmth in his eyes that makes my heart ache. "You were incredible."

I can't stop the tears now, and I don't want to. This moment, with my brother here, with Ethan by my side—it's more than I ever could have dreamed. Lou hasn't ever heard me play since I started violin after her went to prison, and to have him here, now, in one of the most important moments of my life…it's overwhelming in the best way possible.

I turn to Ethan, my heart hammering in my chest.

He smiles, stepping forward to pull me into a soft embrace. "I'm so proud of you, Arya."

I don't even know how to thank him for getting me this opportunity. After I failed my audition so badly, I was certain my dreams of playing in Carnegie Hall were over, but Ethan was determined to make them happen. Through some of his connections, he got me an audition as an opener for the band playing here tonight, and instead of being one among many in an orchestra, I just had the solo performance of my life on that stage. I hold him tightly, letting the tears fall. This is everything. My dreams, my family, and the man I love—all coming together in a way I never thought possible.

After we finally pull apart, Lou claps me on the shoulder, his grin wide.

"You've got a fan for life now," he teases, and I laugh, wiping at my eyes.

"Better late than never," I shoot back, grinning through the tears.

Later, after the rush of the evening begins to settle, we head out, the three of us—me, Lou, and Ethan—together like a little family. As we walk through the bustling streets of New York, I realize that this is just the beginning.

In a few days, I'll be heading out on my next tour with Ethan by my side. There's so much ahead of us, so much to look forward to, but for now, I'm exactly where I need to be.

As we walk, Ethan takes my hand, squeezing it gently.

"Remember when you asked what I wanted to do with my

life?" he asks, his eyes gleaming. "This. This is it. Loving you, making a life with you… It's everything."

I smile up at my husband, my heart full and my future bright.

When I married this man, it was nothing more than a contract. An arrangement that was mutually beneficial with a clear end point.

Now, I never want it to end. The love between us is real, and I can't imagine my life without Ethan in it. He's my forever, and I'm looking forward to every moment of our lives together and the family we've already started to build.

Turn the page for a sneak peek of Fake To Forever!

About Fake To Forever

Nothing is ever simple…not even if it's fake.

It should have been a simple arrangement.

Christian Tallow is new in town. A single dad whose son is in my kindergarten class.

He is broody, uncertain, kind, and would do anything for his son.

So what if he also looks like my book boyfriend come to life?

Christian needed to show the judge that his son has a strong woman figure in his life, ensuring his ex couldn't get custody.

I just needed to make my mom's last dream come true. One that would see her little girl married before she was gone.

Saying yes to a fake marriage seemed like a win-win.

It should have been a simple proposal. But nothing could stay simple forever.

Good thing this was fake from the start.

Right?

Chapter One: Haven

OIL RIGS AND DYING MOTHERS

"SO... WHAT did the doctor say today?"

The question causes me to flinch. I'd anticipated it, of course, but I hate having to answer. Releasing a long sigh, I look up to meet my brother's dark green gaze.

"He said it was just a matter of time now," I murmur, clutching my glass of beer so hard, my fingers turn white. "All we can do is make mom as comfortable as possible."

Gary sucks in a deep breath and then lets it out in a long whoosh before taking a drink. "Shit. I was afraid of that."

"There's a chance she won't make it until after you're back," I say

He nods, his scruffy jaw tensing. "Yeah, I figured as much. They'll let me come back early if I have to, though, so don't worry about that."

I lift my head higher and reach out to snag his arm in my hand, unable to hold back my relief.

"Really? I didn't think the oil fields would be that flexible for you."

He shrugs. "It'd be different if I was on an off-shore rig, but since I'm inland, it's easier."

Thank God! I feel like a bit of the weight on my shoulders

has been lifted. His boss acts like the rest of the world doesn't exist outside of the oil fields when Gary's out there, so I've been scared he wouldn't let my brother go if things with Mom took a turn while he was away.

"How's Peter doing?" Gary asks.

Peter, our stepfather, is so over the moon in love with our mom. I know her death will devastate him. I don't want to put any more stress on Gary's shoulders, though, so I don't tell him how Peter barely kept it together after the doctor gave Mom's final prognosis.

"As good as can be expected, I guess. Losing mom is obviously going to be hard for him, but he was putting on a brave front today."

"Peter's good." Gary shrugs, dropping his gaze from mine. "He's always been good. You've always been good too, Haven. You're better than me, especially when it comes to Mom. I know I should've been there today, but I just...you know..."

"I do know." Reaching out to squeeze his arm, I try to offer what comfort I can. "Don't worry, I get it. It's a lot, but you promise you'll see Mom before you leave, right?"

"Of course." His voice trembles. It's barely discernible, but I pick up on it. I know him too well. It's hard for him to see Mom suffering. Gary's the type of guy who sees a problem and wants to fix it, but he can't fix Mom. He's also not good at dealing with feelings of helplessness. "I just didn't want to be there and listen to the doctor tell us there wasn't any more hope."

We fall into silence as we sip our beers. What more is there to say, really? Even though I'm on the verge of tears, I hold them back. Crying never solved anything, and I don't want to make Gary feel worse than he already does. If I can focus on the soft murmur of the bar's activities around me, I can hold out and delay my breakdown until later, when I'm alone and away from my brother.

Besides, I can't let my emotions ruin this time together. It's tradition that before Gary goes off for his month-long shift in the nearby oil fields, we come to our favorite spot, *Carson's*, and sit at the bar together to get beer-drunk before he goes off to join his fellow roughnecks.

Living in Blue Ridge Falls, Texas, roughnecks are everywhere. Plenty of oil magnates reside in this state, and some even come from the off-shore rig in the Gulf, working inland until the off-shore rig has some new work for them.

Roughnecks are, by and large, young, wiry guys with muscular forearms, tattoos, and sometimes less than spotless backgrounds. My giant of a brother fits that description to a T, apart from the shady past. He towers over me with his 6'2" height and wide, muscular frame. His dark hair and closely cropped beard give him a rugged appearance, and he has a reputation for being a total playboy, since the girls seem to throw themselves at him.

Which…you know. Gross.

Gary finishes his beer and then waves the bartender, a burly man who looks more like a lumberjack than a bartender, over to order another one.

"Did I tell you my friend Christian is moving into town?"

The topic change is abrupt, but not worth bringing attention to. It's hard enough for both of us.

"Your friend from college? The billionaire? Why the hell would he move to Blue Ridge?"

"He wants a quieter life." Gary shrugs. "The peaceful small town experience, you know?"

I roll my eyes. "Ah, I gotcha."

What Gary really means is his rich buddy decided he wants to come to our town, build a monstrosity of a house that he'll call his 'country home', and spend a couple weekends out of the year here when he gets bored of the city. Typical.

Gary absentmindedly scratches at the stubble on his cheek. "Yeah, he's coming to town next week. I'll be in the fields by then, but once I'm back, I want you two to finally meet." 'Finally meet' has an undertone I'm not thrilled about.

"Oh, yeah?" I chuckle. "Don't tell me you're going to try and hook me up with your rich, pretentious middle-aged friend, Gary. I've already told you, I'm not…"

"I'm not trying to hook you up with anyone," he insists. But I know him better than that, and it's not like this wouldn't be the first time.

"Oh, sure. You just want us to meet for shits and giggles."

Gary nods to the bartender when his beer is placed in front of him, frowning at me before he takes a drink. "I promise you, I've no intention of hooking you two up…and he's not middle-aged. He's just a guy, and he's not going to hit on you, so you don't need to worry about that."

"Good. Because I'm not looking to date any stuck-up oil magnate nepo baby."

"You have such a weird thing against rich people," Gary mutters.

"It's not weird! We grew up with practically nothing. People like your friend are born with a silver spoon in their mouths and they don't appreciate anything."

Gary's back stiffens, and he doesn't look at me when he says, "Christian's worked hard for what he has."

I know Gary's just defending his friend, but I don't back down. "How hard do you have to work if daddy gives you your first job?"

Never one to let things bother him for too long, Gary takes another swig of his beer, shaking his head. "I guess we'll just have to agree to disagree."

I scowl at him, playing with the little bowl of peanuts between us. Finding the biggest one, I chuck it at his head, and laugh when it bounces off and lands in his beard. Gary's always taken care of me, been the best big brother anyone could ask for. Growing up poor in a small town like Blue Ridge was hard, but Gary made sure I had what I needed, and even a few things I wanted by taking extra shifts or working odd jobs. That was before he became head honcho of the inland rig just north of Blue Ridge.

Maybe he's a little overprotective, but he's a good big brother.

Not that I'm going to tell him that. He has a big enough head already.

Suppose I should trust his judgment when it comes to his friends. I don't really understand why or how he became friends with the likes of Christian Tallow to begin with–outside of them both going to the same college. Tallow is a billionaire oil tycoon who could not have grown up more different from us. We worked our asses off just to get by, and Tallow came from a wealthy family who helped him build his own massive wealth.

The bar's front door opens and a group of four guys come inside, talking and laughing loudly. I spare them a glance, but that's about it. Since half the town works on the rigs, it's a safe assumption they're roughnecks. They make their way toward the pool tables on the other side of the bar, and I turn back to Gary. He's watching me with an arched brow and a small grin playing around his lips.

"What?" I demand to know, frowning. "Why are you looking at me like that?"

"You want to go talk to those guys?" A smirk plays behind the lip of his beer.

"That is such a weird thing for you to say." I turn back around on my stool, effectively tuning the group out. Definitely not interested.

"What? Is it so wrong for me to want to see my baby sister settled and happy? To actually go out with a guy and have a little fun once in a while?"

"I appreciate your concern, Gary, but I'm fine. I don't need anyone right now. Between work and taking care of Mom, I'm too busy, anyway."

The look he sends my way tells me he's not letting this go

anytime soon. And I have a feeling I'm not going to like what he says next.

"What are you going to do when Mom isn't around anymore?" he asks.

The question makes my stomach twist so hard, bile rises up my throat, but I manage to swallow it back down and push away the fear and pain that his words provoke.

"I'll figure it out," I say, my words weak even to my own ears. "I'm an adult, Gary. I can manage my life on my own."

"But you shouldn't have to." He slams his bottle down with a little more force, causing a few peanuts to fall out of the bowl. "You should have a family of your own and a life outside of our family's tiny bubble. It's what you've always wanted."

"Look who's talking," I reply, slapping on a grin to hide the effect what he's saying is having on me. "Am I really getting this lecture from my workaholic brother who gets bored with a girl so quickly, she doesn't last more than a couple of dates?"

"Yeah, well, I'm not exactly the family type," he says. He looks away, a shadow falling over his eyes, but I'm too fired up to deal with his own insecurities.

"You do realize how hypocritical that is, right?"

Gary grumbles under his breath a moment before replying, "whatever. I just worry about you, okay? I know Mom worries, too. We just don't want you to be lonely."

I appreciate his concern, I really do. But I'm not a little kid anymore. But now's not the time or the place. He'll be leaving soon, and I'll miss him. No point spending what little time we have left arguing. "Don't worry about me. I'm fine. I'm very happy with my life, and if I decide someday that I want the whole marriage, kids, and white picket fence. I'll make it happen."

Gary smirks and shakes his head. "You make it sound so easy, but I know you, Haven. If you do decide to give your heart to someone, he's going to have to be someone extraordinary. Someone who isn't from Blue Ridge. The world is much bigger than this place, and you belong out in it."

His words warm my heart, but I don't let him know that. I lift my glass to take a long drink, not wanting Gary to see the effect his statement is having on me. He's right. The world is much bigger than Blue Ridge, but this town is what I know and where I feel safe. It's where my family is. Venturing outside of Blue Ridge would open me up to all the heartbreak and dangers the rest of the world holds. I've experienced enough pain in my life, and I'm not interested in going out and inviting more in.

Blue Ridge is where I belong, and I just need to keep on focusing on the things that matter most to me so that I don't lose them. My family, my friends, and my job. I don't need more than that. Gary might not get it, even if I fully explained it to him, but that's okay. I don't need him to understand. I just need him to come back from the oil fields safe and sound.

If I can maintain what I already have and the people I already care about, I'll never have to let anything or anyone else in...so I won't have to worry about losing anyone else either.

Want to keep reading? Scan the QR code below to download Fake To Forever!

Subscribe to my newsletter to stay up to date on all things Noelle Stone!

Follow me on social media and join my Facebook group for sneak peeks into what's coming next!

AUTHOR BIO:

She's the literary architect of dashing billionaires and sassy, sweet heroines, adding heart-pounding twists and turns to every tale.

Her castle is filled with her loyal husband and the feline rockstar, Freddie Mercury Jr.

When she's not conjuring love stories, you'll catch her conquering the waves with her dragon boat crew, turning every adventure into a page-turner!

9 781966 960003